# PROMISE ME FOREVER

# PROMISE ME FOREVER

•

# CHARLOTTE DUDLEY

*AVALON BOOKS*
THOMAS BOUREGY AND COMPANY, INC.
401 LAFAYETTE STREET
NEW YORK, NEW YORK 10003

PRINTED IN THE UNITED STATES OF AMERICA
ON ACID-FREE PAPER
BY HADDON CRAFTSMEN, SCRANTON, PENNSYLVANIA

To my Monday night writing group: Charlene, Elaine, Arlene, Bobbie Sue, and Sharon—Thanks

## Chapter One

Lisa nervously chewed her lip as the shuttle van zipped away from Sea-Tac International airport and headed down I–5 towards Tacoma. Still a jumble of nerves from the trip to Portland and the events of the last few days she was unable to relax. Leaning back into the seat she willed herself to unwind. With slender fingers she smoothed the hair at the sides of her head, which was pulled back and tied with a soft pink ribbon. Then, absentmindedly, she patted the dark fringe of bangs framing her big gray-blue eyes. Her effort, however, did not erase the minute frown from her forehead.

With a sigh, she glanced over at her thirteen-year-old brother who sat next to her reading a current issue of *Mad* magazine. As a first grade teacher she was experienced in dealing with young children, but she knew nothing about teenagers. In fact, her stomach did flip-flops every time she thought about her new role as Todd's guardian.

A strong sense of protectiveness filled her as she continued to watch Todd. Although he wasn't her blood brother Lisa's love for the teenager was genuine. Besides, Lisa saw this as her opportunity to repay the Bowmans for adopting her into their home so many years ago, and for the love they had generously and unconditionally given her.

Due to the twelve-year difference in their ages, Lisa's role had always been that of a 'big sister' rather than confidant, and now, the death of their mother had placed her in that position again. Since their Dad had died in a fire several years earlier that left Lisa to see after Todd until he turned eighteen, and she was determined to make his time with her comfortable and secure.

Lisa sat on the modern sofa scanning the classified ads, in search of a bigger apartment. Six days had passed since she and Todd had arrived in Tacoma, and already her one-bedroom duplex was closing in on them. They were constantly bumping into one another. Their adjustment was turning out to be more difficult than she expected, and they certainly didn't need the additional stress of tight quarters.

It was obvious Todd resented her role as an authoritative figure, and she was beginning to feel like a failure. "You're my sister, not my jailer," he accused, when she was laying out rules for his curfew.

Gathering her wandering thoughts Lisa focused her eyes back to the fine print of the paper. Column after column, it was the same thing. There was nothing available for rent that suited their needs or that she could afford.

Sighing, Lisa looked around at the small duplex. Unless a bigger place miraculously became available, it looked as though they were going to be here for a while. She eyed the modest furnishings in the small living room. Perhaps if she rearranged the furniture she could squeeze a chest in here for her clothes? And if she got rid of everything that wasn't necessary, maybe it would give the illusion of more space?

A knock at the door interrupted her woolgathering. Todd? She'd had a key made for him the day after they arrived, but he never remembered to put it in his pocket. Tossing aside the newspaper, she pushed away from the sofa and went to the door.

Out of habit she peeked out the small fan-shaped viewing window. It wasn't Todd. Instead she caught a glimpse of a firm forehead with a wave of sable brown hair combed neatly to the side.

Probably a salesman, she thought, who had conveniently missed the *no soliciting* sign posted on the building. Well, whatever he was selling—be it vacuum cleaners or encyclopedias—she wasn't interested. She needed to thin out her possessions, not add to them.

Not in the mood for a showdown with a slick vendor, Lisa opened the door slowly. The words 'I'm not interested' were on the tip of her tongue. When she was face to face with the man on her porch, she stood there mouth open. Her brief glance through the viewing window hadn't done the man justice. Instead of a shark in a polyester suit, she found herself face to face with a very appealing man dressed in a khaki shirt and chinos.

He was about thirty years old, and although not handsome, his jutting chin, sensual lips and intense hazel eyes gave him a mysterious attractive appearance. Lisa swallowed. If his sales pitch was half as interesting, well . . . she might own a new vacuum cleaner before the afternoon was over.

Feeling her resolve slipping, Lisa smiled and pointed to the *no soliciting* sign off to his right. At his stern look, her smile faded.

"Lisa Bowman?" As the stranger spoke her name, Todd stepped forward.

Lisa gasped. Something was definitely wrong here. "Todd, are you all right?"

When Todd nodded, Lisa's gaze slid back to the man. "Is . . . there a problem?" Her voice was barely audible.

With what appeared to be a forced smile, the man produced a wallet and flicked it open. "Detective Grant Harper, with the Tacoma Police department," announced the deep resonant voice. "I'm off duty right now," he said, as if to explain his casual attire. "Although this isn't an official visit, I hope we can talk."

After a quick examination of the identification he held out, Lisa nodded and moved aside, allowing Todd to pass. Detective Harper followed, his tall, lean frame barely clearing the doorway. The man dwarfed her five feet eight inches, making her feel small and vulnerable.

"Please sit down," Lisa invited, indicating the sofa. Then she turned to Todd. "Perhaps you should wait in your room. That is, unless Detective Harper wants you to stay?"

Detective Harper gave Lisa a courteous smile. Then he nodded at Todd. "I've already spoken to Todd, you're the one I want to see." His tone seemed gentler now, and Lisa relaxed somewhat as Todd left the room.

Detective Harper waited for Lisa to sit before taking a seat on the sofa across from her. "Todd's really a pretty nice kid. He just needs a little guidance."

Lisa met his gaze. "Surely you haven't stopped by just to tell me this?" Although her heart was beating wildly, her voice was firm. She would not be intimidated by the man, nor would she turn into a frightened mouse.

"Of course not. But before we get off on the wrong foot, let me put your mind at ease. Todd's not in any trouble, and I'm not here to cause any problems." He paused.

Lisa exhaled the breath she was holding. Todd wasn't in trouble. The tightness in her limbs faded and she leaned back.

"However, if he continues to associate

with the kids I found him with, I'm sure his luck will run out."

This last comment was like a blast from a cold shower, and Lisa sprang to her brother's defense. "He's only been in Tacoma six days. I hardly think that's enough time to be associating with ... with anyone."

"That may be, Miss Bowman, but the boys he was with today have all been in some kind of hassle with the law."

"Well, just what is it my brother's done?"

"He and three other boys were setting off illegal firecrackers."

"Firecrackers ... Is that all?"

"These weren't just firecrackers, Miss Bowman, but illegal ones. In case you haven't noticed the paper's reported several potentially dangerous incidents involving illegal fireworks."

Lisa felt her cheeks warm. No, she hadn't noticed, she'd been too busy poring over the classified ads in search of an apartment.

"Besides property damage, someone could have been hurt," Detective Harper continued. "Every year a kid loses an eye or a finger or two to these illegal pyrotechnics."

"Are you sure Todd was with these other boys?" Lisa asked hopefully. "Isn't it just possible he was an innocent bystander?"

"I'm afraid not Miss Bowman. I was flying my model plane on the vacant school yard and I had a good view of what was going on. He was definitely part of the group."

Her hopes fell. "I see."

"Even though school is out for the summer and they were setting them off in the vacant parking lot, the weather conditions have been too dry to take any chances. It's best if we can stop this type of thing before it gets out of hand."

Tight-lipped, Lisa forced herself to speak. "I'll talk to Todd about the dangers of illegal pyrotechnics," came her stiff reply. She knew she should be grateful for his concern, but his lecture had caught her off balance. Besides, he was a little overbearing for her liking.

The man gave her a wry smile. "You know, it's not just the fireworks, Miss Bowman, it's Todd. He needs a little direction from an adult. He shouldn't—"

Every nerve in Lisa's body sprang to attention. She leaned forward, her chin lifted with stubborn indignation. "I think I fit that category," she interrupted, not giving him a chance to continue. She knew she looked young for her age, but did he think she was a mere teenager? He was presuming a lot.

"I don't need someone who plays with toy airplanes to lecture me on being an adult," Lisa ground out between clenched teeth.

"I apologize if I upset you. I wasn't inferring you aren't an adult." He met her gaze without flinching. "I'd just hate to see a nice kid like Todd influenced to take the wrong path."

"I . . . I'll talk to him about that too," Lisa stammered. Then before she knew what was happening all her pent up emotions came pouring out. "I'm afraid Todd doesn't pay much attention to me. We . . . we seem to be having a communication gap. We're both having a time adjusting to our new circumstances." Her eyes shone with unshed tears.

"I know," he said sympathetically. "Todd explained everything on the way here. The problem is, things are going to get worse if he doesn't receive the proper guidance. Todd could probably use a man's influence. Is there a neighbor, or a boyfriend who can help?"

Off hand Lisa couldn't think of any one. There was Ralph, he was a professor of archaeology at a local university, and they had been dating rather steadily for the past year, but he was away on a dig. "No one," she said, shaking her head in frustration.

"I see. If you wouldn't think me a buttin-sky, maybe I could help."

"You'd be willing to do that?"

"Yes, I would. I'd be glad to act as a big brother if Todd needs a man to talk to. I'll also introduce him to some of the kids down at the recreational center."

Meeting the warm hazel eyes measuring her from across the room, Lisa felt an unexplainable surge of . . . She wasn't sure how to describe the feeling that washed over her. Maybe it was contentment, or maybe she was simply grateful for the offer of help. Suddenly the world seemed a whole lot brighter. "That would be very nice, but when would you have the time? And why would you want to bother?"

His mouth curved upwards into a boyish grin. "I'd make the time. As to why, I guess I see a little of myself in Todd. Having lost my father when I was twelve I feel as though I can relate to his circumstances. And, if it hadn't been for a conscientious police chaplain I might be on the other side of the law today, myself." His tawny eyes seemed to light up with memories.

A faint smile formed on Lisa's lips and a new-found respect for the man wiggled its way into her heart. "Are you sure we won't be imposing, Mr. Harper? And ... I couldn't pay you very much."

His chuckle was deep and rich. "I don't exactly see you as threatening me into acquiescence. And the only payment I want is for you to drop this Mr. stuff and call me Grant."

Those eyes, and that deep voice of his seemed to be having a hypnotic affect upon her. "Of course, Grant," Lisa said turning away. She hoped to break the spell she found herself under. When she looked into Grant's face again, she felt more in control of herself.

For a second it seemed that neither she nor Grant knew what to say to the other, and the silence filling the room grew to an almost explosive level before Grant spoke.

He was glancing at the newspaper she had tossed aside earlier. "Looking for an apartment?"

The sound of his voice startled her out of her stupor. "Why, yes. As a matter of fact I am, but I'm not having much luck."

"How particular are you? Do you need a swimming pool and all the extras?"

Lisa raised one perfectly arched brow. "Not with my budget. I really have only three requirements. First, it can't be too far from this area. Second, it needs two bed-rooms, and lastly, the rent has to be rea-sonable."

"I know of a place like that." Taking paper and pencil from his shirt pocket, Grant wrote down a name and telephone number, then in two easy strides, crossed the room and pressed the paper into her hand. "I've an inside tip this place is going to be avail-able in a few days. You might want to check it out."

"Thanks." Lisa looked at the paper then slipped it into the pocket of her jeans. "Are you sure you're not a miracle worker in dis-guise?"

Grant gave an amused laugh. "I've been called a lot of things, but never a miracle worker," he assured her.

"Maybe you should consider changing professions," she teased. "It's probably safer than police work." Was it her imagination, or did his jaw tighten at her remark?

She hadn't meant to offend him. Lisa was glad there were men willing to risk their lives for the public, but a fact was a fact. Policemen, like firefighters, put their lives on the line daily. Memories of a scene ten years ago rushed in upon her.

They had just gone to bed when a knock

sounded at the door. Upon recognizing the fire chief from Mr. Bowman's station, the family knew instinctively what the caller wanted. She and Grant had something in common; they both had lost their fathers when they were young.

Grant cleared his throat, rousing Lisa from her reverie. "Please excuse me," she apologized, disgusted with herself for her poor manners. "I didn't mean to ignore you. I'm afraid I'm a hopeless dreamer at times."

He gave her an understanding smile. "That's quite all right, but I've really taken too much of your time as it is. If you'll allow me to say goodbye to Todd, I'll be on my way."

Had she offended him? His request seemed a little abrupt. Lisa pointed toward the short hallway. "The bedroom is the second door on the left."

From where she was sitting Lisa could see Grant knock on the bedroom door and exchange words with Todd before returning to the living room.

"I told Todd we'd go for a soda tomorrow and he seemed interested," Grant said.

Appreciative of all his help, Lisa extended her hand. "I . . . I want to thank you again for your offer to spend time with Todd."

For a moment Grant just looked at her and Lisa thought she was going to melt under his magnetic gaze. And the warmth of his hand shake was equally disturbing. For a fleeting minute Lisa was reminded of what an attractive man Grant Harper was.

"I've got to be going, Lisa. Don't forget to call that number I gave you," Grant said, stepping outside. Lisa watched, a smile on her face, as he walked towards an aged station wagon parked at the curb.

Closing the door, Lisa leaned against the cool hard wood, a pleased look on her face. To think that only moments earlier she thought she had an encyclopedia salesman to contend with. Instead, Grant Harper might turn out to be that miracle she needed. And an attractive miracle at that.

## Chapter Two

Lisa walked to the phone, eager to check on the apartment Grant had told her about. If she was lucky it would still be available.

Todd entered the room as she started dialing. "I'm sorry, Lisa. I didn't mean to cause you any trouble. It's just that I don't know anyone here and I feel kinda lost. Grant told me about those kids and the trouble they've been in. I promise to stay away from them."

This was a new side of Todd that Lisa hadn't witnessed before. Returning the phone to its cradle, she wrapped her arms around her brother and hugged him. "It's okay honey. We'll work things out between us. We just need a little more time."

When she looked at Todd's face he looked much younger than his years. Lisa drew him near and hugged him again. "I'm glad Grant came along when he did, however, before someone was hurt or before any property was damaged."

Todd pulled away from Lisa's embrace and gave her an apologetic smile, then with a quick mood change, asked, "Isn't he neat?"

Lisa didn't need to ask who *He* was. Todd was thoroughly in awe of Grant Harper.

Todd was only three-years-old at the time of John Bowman's death and it was obvious he missed his Dad. Lisa knew he needed a male role model; someone he could be close to and confide in.

Slipping her hand into the pocket of her jeans she felt the piece of paper Grant had given her. "Why don't you go in the kitchen and fix yourself some lunch. There's tuna in the refrigerator and a bag of chips on the counter. I'm going to call about an apartment. It sounds just like what we need, so keep your fingers crossed."

Todd held up both his hands with his forefingers crossed. "Good luck."

Lisa gave him a playful tap on the shoulder. Maybe she'd get the hang of this parenting thing yet.

An impish grin creased Todd's mouth. "Thanks for not getting angry," he said heading for the kitchen.

Lisa was about to hang up the phone when someone on the other end of the line picked it up on the fifth ring and giggled into the receiver.

"Hello, Marilyn? I'm Lisa Bowman. I was talking with Grant Harper and he said your apartment might be available soon."

"That's right," answered the faceless Marilyn. Then there was another burst of giggles, "I'm out of here in two more days."

"I was wondering if I might stop by and see the place?" Actually she was almost willing to take it sight unseen if it had two bedrooms and if the rent was reasonable.

"Of course." Then there was a giggle. "But could you make that about six this evening, I'm kind of busy right now."

Lisa could imagine how Marilyn was busy, she had caught the sound of a man's voice in the background. "Six will be fine," she agreed, "but I'll need your address."

Replacing the phone, Lisa looked down just as the mail came fluttering through the mail slot.

Scooping it off the tan carpeting, Lisa took a seat on the sofa and fanned through the assortment of flyers and various pieces of junk mail until she came to a letter from Ralph.

A twinge of shame stabbed at her conscience. She had been so busy since Ralph's departure two weeks ago, that she had given him little thought.

Before leaving for her mother's funeral, Lisa had called Ralph to explain she wouldn't be able to see him off on his trip. He was participating in an archaeological dig sponsored by a university back east, and wouldn't be returning until the end of July. She had promised to accompany him to the airport to see him off, but that was before learning of her mother's death.

Ralph had been disappointed when he heard she couldn't make it, but of course, he didn't blame her for the unexpected turn of events. Still, she knew by the sound of his voice he had been somewhat perturbed by her change in plans.

Although they had been dating for a year theirs was not a serious romance, but with time Lisa felt certain she would grow to love Ralph. He was intelligent, handsome, and quite charming when he wanted to be, and Lisa enjoyed his company. And, Ralph seemed to be satisfied with the way their relationship was going.

Already in a somewhat melancholy mood, a surge of loneliness engulfed Lisa when she looked down at Ralph's letter. Did absence—as the old saying goes—make the heart grow fonder? She quickly tore open the white envelope bearing her name and written in Ralph's precise handwriting.

*Dear Lisa,*

*I do believe I was the only person departing in my group who didn't have a wife or sweetheart to see him off. I'll have to admit I felt somewhat like a lost puppy. Don't get me wrong, I know you had no control over what happened, but I just hope I'm not put in such an embarrassing situation again.*

*Being alone with no one to see me off did open my eyes to one thing. YOU'VE BECOME VERY SPECIAL TO ME. I think it's time we reexamine our future plans. As mother says, I need to find the right girl and settle down, and I think you're the right one for me. After all, we've dated for a year, and I think it's time we made a commitment to each other.*

Surprised by Ralph's candor, Lisa stared at the letter in her hand. She hadn't expected their relationship to reach this level so soon. She cared for Ralph a great deal, but was she ready for commitment? After all, she had Todd to think about now.

Lisa read the rest of Ralph's letter—he wrote about his work and the anticipation of finding some important link with the past—but her mind kept slipping back to the first page; second paragraph.

Had they finally crossed the line between friendship and marriage? After giving the matter more thought Lisa found the idea of marrying Ralph quite enticing. Perhaps their union would provide the support that Todd needed so badly right now? Then she wouldn't have to seek help from a total stranger—such as Grant Harper.

She smiled tentatively. Yes, Ralph's proposal might just be the answer to her problem with Todd, and she felt certain Ralph would make a good husband. Several women at the university where Ralph taught envied her and would give anything to be in her position. If she turned down his offer she could be replaced in a blink of an eye.

The more she thought about marrying

Ralph the more she liked the idea. A husband and family had always been her dream and Ralph's job as a professor wasn't dangerous so she would feel emotionally secure. That was important. She could not stand to be like her mother, always worrying about her husband's safety.

If she were to marry someone like Grant Harper, she'd be worried all the time. Now where did that thought come from?

Pushing thoughts of the good-looking detective from her mind, Lisa quickly penned a letter to Ralph, assuring him she would meet his plane and was anxious for his return. As she placed the stamp on the envelope, Lisa took a moment to picture herself walking down the aisle in a beautiful white gown towards the figure waiting at the altar. Although she strained for a clearer image of the groom's face, one wouldn't come. But the shadow cast against the altar was that of a tall man.

Concentrating on her steps, she moved with the music, closing the distance that separated them. Soon she would see his face. Suddenly the music grew louder abruptly breaking the spell. Faltering, Lisa lost her balance and almost fell.

The stumble in her make-believe fantasy

brought her back to the present. Although music was playing, it wasn't the wedding march. This music sounded more like the rantings of a maniac and it was coming from Todd's room.

With a forced smile, and searching for a supply of patience, Lisa tramped down the hall, knocking on the bedroom door. "Todd, could you please turn that-that . . . music down."

"Oh, sorry," Todd said opening the door.

In spite of his sincerity, Lisa shook her head, knowing that tomorrow she'd have to remind him again.

"By the way, I need to go to the store. Then I'm going to look at that apartment I was telling you about. Do you want to come along?"

Todd shook his head. "Go ahead without me. There's a science fiction movie coming on TV I'd like to see."

Lisa looked at her watch. "Okay. I won't be long. Don't get into any trouble while I'm gone."

"Ah, Sis, I told you there's a movie on TV I want to see. How can I get in trouble watching television?"

Ignoring this remark, Lisa turned to go. "I'll fix dinner when I get home."

After a stop at a nearby supermarket to replenish a supply of nonperishable items, Lisa drove to the address Marilyn had given her. Before getting out of her car Lisa studied the neighborhood. The houses and yards were well maintained which she considered a good sign. There was a basketball hoop attached above the double garage and the house across the street had a couple of skateboards in the driveway. This could only mean one thing, someone close to Todd's age lived there. Another good sign.

From the outside the duplex appeared to be just what she wanted, nothing fancy, but definitely clean and well maintained. Exiting her car she hurried up the walk.

Each unit had a big picture window facing the street and they were linked by separate garages. The building was painted a dark brown with a tan trim which she didn't consider very appealing—she much preferred lighter, brighter colors—but at least the paint wasn't faded or peeling. Anxious to see the inside, Lisa rang the bell.

"You're right on time," said the perky blonde who opened the door.

Lisa suppressed her smile. Except for being younger than she had pictured, Marilyn was just what she had expected, a well-stacked, kooky blonde.

"I do appreciate you letting me drop in like this. I won't take much of your time."

"No problem. You'll just have to excuse the mess." Marilyn gestured toward the boxes crowded about the room. "I would have finished packing today, but my boy-friend came over, and he's more interesting than this boring job." She rolled her eyes and giggled.

"Well it's very nice of you to let me interrupt your packing," Lisa replied, moving inside.

Having recovered from her fit of giggles, Marilyn stepped back. "Ready to look around?"

The tour was quick, but Lisa saw everything she needed to see. The place suited her fine. "I'll take it," she said, trying to restrain her enthusiasm. "I just hope I'm not too late."

"Don't worry," Marilyn informed her. "I'm sure the place is yours if you want it. All you have to do is go next door and let the owner know."

"The owner lives next door?"

"You didn't know?"

Lisa shook her head. She hoped living

next door to the owner wouldn't prove awkward. She'd heard tales of prying landlords.

Marilyn gave her a funny look, then smiled. "I know he's home. I heard the varoom of that little beast of his pull into the drive just seconds ago."

"Then perhaps I'd better go speak to him before he rents the place to someone else."

Thanking Marilyn for her time Lisa let herself out. As she closed the door, she had to admit Marilyn had turned out to be very nice. If the landlord/neighbor was as friendly the place would be perfect.

The beast Marilyn referred to was a sleek red sports car and was parked on the other side of the drive.

Lisa gave the car an admiring appraisal, then rang the bell to the other unit. Her last thought before the door opened was to wonder if the owner of the beast and the duplex was Marilyn's boyfriend.

As if expecting her ring, the door was promptly opened.

"You!"

Lisa stood on the small portico, her mouth open in surprise. "You own this place?"

Grant gave her a sheepish grin. "Yes."

Annoyance washed over her. What kind of game was he playing?

"I thought you were a police officer." Lisa verbalized her thoughts without thinking.

"I am," Grant answered. "But that doesn't keep me from owning this duplex."

This was true, but why hadn't he told her? She needed an apartment, but she wasn't in the mood for games. "Would you mind explaining." Her request was just short of an order.

A charming smile flashed across Grant's face as he stepped back to allow her to enter, but Lisa didn't budge. His smile died on his face. "It's perfectly safe," he said, giving her a chance to reconsider.

She hadn't meant to come across as doubting his integrity; she just wanted some answers. Straightening her shoulders, Lisa looked Grant straight in the eyes. Her exasperation faded, however, as she gazed into their warm hazel depths. She immediately felt humbled. "I . . . thank you."

Inside, Lisa looked quickly around before taking a seat on the brown tweed sofa.

Grant sat across from her in a leather recliner. "I suppose I do owe you an explanation," he said. "But first, may I get you something to drink? Coffee, tea, or cola," he added hastily.

A tiny smile forced its way onto Lisa's

face. Grant was trying hard to be the proper gentleman and to put her at ease. "A cola will be fine."

While he was getting their drinks Lisa scanned the living and dining rooms, but there wasn't a thing outstanding or out of the ordinary about the place. A model airplane was parked in the middle of the dining table, but other than that, there was nothing that would give her any insight into Grant Harper.

"Here you go," Grant said, handing her a glass. He settled back into the recliner. "Now—where should I start?"

By now, Lisa had begun to relax and her earlier anger along with her doubts had all but evaporated. "Why didn't you tell me this afternoon that you owned this place?" Her voice was soft and low.

"I guess . . . I was afraid of coming on too strong. I'd already offered to help you with Todd. It seemed a little too convenient— even to me—that I just happened to own a duplex too. I didn't want you to say no before looking at it." He gave her an appealing half-smile.

Lisa uttered a self-conscious "Oh."

If Grant was aware of her discomfort he

aptly ignored it. "Well . . . how did you like the place?"

"It was very nice."

"Then you'll be taking it?"

They hadn't even discussed the rent. "I— I'm not sure."

Grant held his palms up. "I'm sorry. I didn't mean to sound pushy. Take all the time you want to think it over."

"Oh, I don't need more time," Lisa said with a resolute shake of her head. "It's perfect, but we haven't discussed the rent."

"Yes, the rent. How much are you paying now?"

Lisa gave him a questioning look, but told him what she was currently paying.

"That will be fine."

A short, unbelievable laugh escaped Lisa's mouth. "Are you sure? I'd feel as though I was taking advantage of you."

"If it will make you feel better, that's ten dollars more than my current tenant pays."

So, Marilyn was getting a low rent too. Lisa's suspicious nature kicked into gear again. Was this man a saint or a devil, and what did he want in return for the low rent?

Grant cleared his throat. "Did anyone ever tell you that you have very expressive eyes? In fact, they're telling me I've been tried and convicted right now."

Taken aback by his frankness, Lisa immediately lowered her gaze.

"I don't need the money," he said in a reassuring voice. "I've got a job. If I can help someone else out, then—why not?"

Lisa looked up and found Grant watching her. His eyes begged her to trust him. "I'll take it," she said, confident she was doing the right thing.

His expression brightened considerably. "Good. I'm going to enjoy having you and Todd for neighbors. Marilyn will be out on Wednesday, so you can move in anytime after that."

"I'll have to see about getting some boxes and renting a truck, but I should be able to move in by the end of the week."

Grant grinned. "If you won't misinterpret my offer, maybe I can help transport some of your things."

Tilting her head back, she gave him an inquiring look. "Somehow, I can't picture the beast as a moving van."

A hearty burst of laughter echoed throughout the room. "I see you've been talking to Marilyn. Well, I wasn't intending to use the ah—beast. I'll use my old station wagon."

Oh yes, Lisa remembered seeing the battered station wagon in front of her place earlier in the day. "Offer accepted. I'll start packing right away. I should be ready by the weekend."

Grant leaned forward. "There's no need to wait. Todd and I could start moving boxes Wednesday evening."

Moving had never been one of Lisa's favorite things to do. The sooner she had it behind her the better. The corners of her mouth lifted into a smile. "That would be great," she replied eagerly.

After another fifteen minutes of casual conversation, Lisa excused herself. "I've really got to be going. Tomorrow is a work day, and I still have to fix dinner tonight."

Grant stood as she rose to leave. "Todd said you're a teacher. I thought teachers had the summer off along with their students."

"Some do, but I volunteered my summer at the Inner-City Community Church reading stories on Tuesdays and Fridays. Actually, it will probably turn out to be more fun than work since I enjoy the little ones."

"That makes you sound fairly dedicated."

There was a hint of admiration in Grant's voice.

"Not to the job, just to the kids. Most of these children are disadvantaged and haven't had the opportunities other kids have had. If I can give them sixty minutes of happiness twice a week, then I'll feel like I've contributed something to this society."

"It still sounds pretty honorable to me."

"No more so than a policeman who's willing to spend his days off helping a teenager stay out of trouble," Lisa reminded him.

Grant tried to shrug off her compliment. "I guess we're more alike than I thought."

For some reason, Grant's statement left her feeling confused. "I must be going," she mumbled.

"I'll see you soon," Grant said, as she reached for the doorknob.

Lisa gave a quick wave and hurried out. She could feel his heated gaze upon her back, but she resisted the urge to turn around.

After slipping behind the steering wheel of her car she sighed and relaxed. She felt as though she had just spent the last few minutes walking a fiery gauntlet and had made it to safety. Grant's presence wasn't physically threatening, but—there was definitely something about the man that caused her pulse to soar and blurred her thinking.

## Chapter Three

"Oh boy, we're having pizza," Todd shouted, eyeing the cardboard box Lisa carried into the kitchen.

Pleased her ploy had worked, Lisa gave Todd a big smile. "My way of apologizing for being gone longer than I expected. Besides, I thought we should celebrate our upcoming move."

"We're moving?"

Lisa didn't miss the hint of concern in Todd's voice or his apprehensive look. She quickly reassured him. "Don't worry, I think you're going to like our new place and our new landlord." As they ate she explained everything to her brother.

Pleased with her news, Todd smiled.

"Gee, Sis, it'll be really neat having Grant as our next door neighbor."

"He does seem like a very likable person." Lisa's voice showed little emotion, but she found herself silently agreeing with Todd.

After dinner Lisa went to the bedroom and picked out a green and white striped dress to wear the next day and hung it in the hall closet.

"Good night," Todd called, as he closed the bedroom door.

"Good night," Lisa answered, stifling a yawn. She wasn't looking forward to all the work involved in moving, but she was definitely anxious to have her own room and her own bed again. The sofa had lost its appeal after the first night.

In no hurry to stretch out on the sofa, Lisa sat down at the contemporary roll-top desk to the left of the front door. She needed to write herself a reminder to stop for boxes on the way home from work tomorrow.

Opening the top drawer, she rummaged through the odds and ends and was ready to give up on finding a pad, when the manila envelope caught her eye. The envelope contained an assortment of papers and pictures that Lisa had brought from her mother's house in Portland.

Unfastening the clasp, she poured the contents out onto the desk. A picture of a shy, frightened little girl of about two landed on top of the pile. The picture had been taken the first day she had come to live with the Bowmans.

From the beginning, Lisa knew she had been adopted, but she was about four before she truly understood what the word meant. But Mom and Dad Bowman had never made her feel the least bit like a stranger. They were a close threesome, and even after Todd was born their love for her never wavered. She owed them so much and missed them both.

Lisa was fifteen when Mr. Bowman died fighting a three-alarm fire at the Brookside apartments. It was a painful loss for a teenager, but the worst part was watching the effect John Bowman's death had on her mother. Oh, she had put on a good front, and her mother had never stopped loving her and Todd or seeing to their needs. But the woman she once had been was buried along with John Bowman. At forty-four Marcia Bowman had become a widow and it didn't seem fair to Lisa.

Her heart ached with loneliness for her deceased parents, but Lisa knew she had to come to grips with her grief. She had Todd to think about now, and she had to be strong for him. And if she could successfully help Todd through the next few years, maybe she'd be able to repay the Bowmans for their love and kindness.

Tears threatened to spill from Lisa's eyes as she quickly shoved the picture and other items back into the big envelope and closed it away in the desk drawer. She couldn't change the past, she had to think about the future. Finding a blank sheet of paper she wrote her note.

Hours later the ringing of the alarm intruded into her sleep. Lisa rose from the couch, grabbed her cotton robe, walked to the window and looked out. The day didn't look very promising. It wasn't raining—yet, but the sky was a murky gray, suggesting a downpour wasn't far off. She sighed, hoping the rain would hold off until after she had moved.

Taking a tan raincoat from the hall closet she slipped it on and retrieved her blue tote, which was stuffed with children's books, from the closet floor.

Todd was in the kitchen eating toast when she came to say goodbye. "I should be home in four or five hours. Behave yourself and don't forget Grant is coming by."

"I won't forget. Why do you think I got up so early?" Todd answered his sister's warning.

"I'll try to get some boxes," Lisa said, ignoring his reply. "Maybe we can get some packing done tonight."

The drive to the Inner-City Community Church took about fifteen minutes, but as Lisa neared her destination an uneasiness, which she couldn't identify, settled in upon her. What was wrong? Surely she wasn't nervous about the prospect of reading to the children?

The signal up ahead flashed from the yellow caution to red and Lisa brought her car to a halt. As she waited for the light to change, she took in her surroundings. Buildings were run down and yards had long ago been forgotten. Vacant houses were boarded up, but much of their protective covering had been ripped away by vagrants or vandals. In fact, the entire area seemed to ooze of despair. It was a depressing sight.

A shudder ran up her spine. How did the people living here survive that feeling of hopelessness? When the signal changed to green, Lisa pressed her foot to the accelerator, eager to reach her destination.

She spotted the white clapboard church up ahead and pulled into the parking area. She was still feeling nervous when she got out of her car. This wasn't the best of neighborhoods.

Gravel crunched beneath her shoes and the sound echoed on the still air, reminding her that she was very much alone. Quickening her pace she hurried up the worn, wooden steps.

At the top of the stairs she paused for only a second then reached for the doorknob and pulled. The door didn't budge. Thinking it was stuck, she tugged again, but to no avail. Panic threatened to envelop her until she realized she was early. Calm down and don't let the morose surroundings spoil your morning, Lisa chastised herself as she retraced her steps.

As she waited in her car for someone to show up, Lisa passed the time by looking over the books she'd brought with her. Before long she was quite engrossed. Preoccupied, she didn't notice the approaching figure. The knock on the window caused her to jump and the books on her lap spilled across the seat. It took several seconds for her pulse to return to normal.

On the other side of the glass, an elderly black lady with beautiful gray hair smiled down at her.

Back in control, Lisa rolled down her window as the woman introduced herself. "I'm Mrs. Mattie Lewis. Are you Lisa Bowman?"

Relieved, Lisa smiled. "Yes, I am."

"Sorry to keep you waiting, dear. But I wanted to get old Tom, my cat, inside, before I left home. Some mornings that cat won't cooperate at all, and this was one of them mornings."

Lisa gave an understanding nod. "I don't think you're late, Mrs. Lewis, I believe I'm the one who's early."

Mattie gave her a face-splitting grin. "That must mean you're eager to get started."

"That I am," said Lisa, getting out of her car.

"Well, come on. I'll give you a quick tour before everyone starts arriving."

Lisa followed Mattie inside the church. She didn't know Mattie's age, but she moved with an ease that belied her gray hair.

From a small vestibule Mattie led the way into the sanctuary lined with wooden pews. "You can use this area for story telling," Mattie suggested, "but if we don't have a very big turnout you can use one of the smaller rooms downstairs."

Lisa smiled her approval.

"I'm so glad to have your help," Mattie was saying, when their conversation was cut short by four exuberant teenage girls, entering the building.

"Hi girls," Mattie called, "Come on over and meet our story reader, Lisa Bowman."

The girls ambled over, chatting among themselves. Lisa smiled at the foursome, pleased to see the respect they showed Mattie by submitting to her request. "Lisa, I want you to meet some more of our volunteers, Dorcas, Alba, Mary and Trish. They'll be helping with the children before story time and during lunch."

Lisa acknowledged each girl then watched as the cheerful teenagers disappeared through a side door. So much planning had obviously gone into the program, she hoped they had a good turnout.

The sound of Mattie's voice penetrated Lisa's thoughts. "By the way, I hope you know you're welcome to stay for lunch."

Since she had so much to do, Lisa was tempted to say "no thanks," but she changed her mind when she looked at Mattie's face. The invitation was not merely an act of courtesy, but was sincerely meant. Lisa's protest died on her lips. Mattie was too sweet to turn down. "I'd love to."

"Good," Mattie replied, reaching over and giving her arm a squeeze. "I like you Lisa Bowman and I think we're going to work well together."

A shy smile spread across Lisa's face. "The feeling is mutual."

Mattie adjusted the skirt of her black and white dress. "You know the kids in this area really don't have a whole lot to look forward to and so many of them end up in trouble. Maybe if we can get to them early enough..." Her voice died out, as if the thought of the lost children was more than she could bear.

Lisa understood Mattie's feelings precisely, as a picture of Todd came to mind. She wanted to erase all the pain and difficulties he'd been through during his young life, and promise him things would improve. It was an impossible promise, of course, for such a declaration might be completely beyond her control. Dabbing at the tears gath-

ering in her eyes she glanced at Mattie, noticing the old lady's eyes were also moist.

"Looks like we're a couple of softies," Mattie said, taking a tissue from her purse and
wiping away her tears. "If everything goes
well, maybe this program can be expanded
next year, but right now I guess we'll have
to take things one day at a time."

"I guess so." Lisa's voice cracked as she
tried gaining her composure. "I'll sure do
what I can to help out."

"That's the spirit," Mattie commended,
before turning back down the aisle.

Lisa was sure she could see the fragile
black lady rubbing her eyes as she moved
away.

Later, as Lisa stood before the group of
twenty children, most of whom were under
the age of five, her stomach quivered with
butterflies and her confidence waned. Her
responsibility seemed overwhelming as she
surveyed her audience. She had only thirty
minutes to transport these kids from an en-
vironment that was often harsh and cruel
into a world of make believe. A world of
escape. If she failed . . . they might not return.

"Good morning boys and girls. I'm your
story reader, Lisa Bowman. This is my first

day on the job and I'm so glad you showed up to help me out."

When the complaisant faces of her audience broke into smiles Lisa sighed, and relaxed. She had hoped for a bigger turnout, but at least the kids were receptive.

Her courage reinforced, Lisa was eager to begin. She removed a book from her canvas tote about a neighborhood parade, hoping the kids could relate to the children in the story and realize that they too could have fun with a minimum of store bought toys. Halfway through the story she noticed signs of restlessness and laid her book down.

"Time for a break," she directed. At first she had the kids stretch towards the ceiling then bend and touch their toes. After that she lined them up, forming their own parade, and they marched around the room twice. When she picked up her book again all signs of unrest had disappeared.

By the time Lisa announced The End and closed the book she felt as though a bond had been formed between herself and the youngsters. She was looking forward to their next story time. If she had done her job well the kids would return, if not . . .

Concerned, Lisa asked how many would return on Friday. When twenty waving hands shot up she breathed a sigh of relief, glad she hadn't let Mattie and the others down. "That's just great, kids. I'll be looking forward to seeing everyone again.

"Right now, I do believe Mrs. Lewis and her helpers have lunch prepared for us, so let's line up in a nice straight row again, and we'll go downstairs."

Mattie intercepted the little parade at the back of the room, her face beaming. "You were terrific," she whispered to Lisa.

"Thanks," Lisa mouthed.

Lunch was a noisy affair that consisted of cheese and crackers, juice, and a cookie. Since most of the kids wanted to sit next to Lisa, she solved the problem by dividing her time between the three tables that were being used.

At one o'clock Lisa excused herself and said goodbye to all her new friends.

Outside, she was glad and surprised to see that the weatherman's forecast for clearing skies and fair weather had held true.

As she drove away she kept looking at the note taped to the dash. She mustn't forget to stop and pick up some boxes. With moving on her mind, she had gone several blocks when she realized her mood had shifted completely from what it had been that morning.

Looking around she realized nothing had changed. It was still the same surroundings, but somehow the drive home didn't seem as bleak. Hope, that's what it is. Now she understood how people like Mattie survived in this neighborhood. Hope was their light at the end of the tunnel. It offered the promise of better things to come.

Her uplifted mood came at the same time as the sun slipped out from behind a cloud, adding to her sense of contentment. Lisa reached over and flipped on the radio and a cheery melody soon filled the car.

She was humming along with the lively tune when she remembered the note taped to the dash and pulled into the shopping center parking lot a mile from her apartment.

"Boxes are crushed early in the morning," she was told everywhere she asked. Disappointed, she walked back to her car empty handed. Tomorrow she would get up with the birds, surely then she would find some boxes before they were flattened.

She was unlocking her car, when a flash of red caught her eye. Turning, Lisa saw a sporty red car pulling into the parking area of the Hometown Restaurant that occupied the northwest corner of the small mall. Could it be? She wasn't very good at identifying cars, but it certainly looked like his car. The chances were slim, but then Grant emerged from the car.

Lisa was just about to shout "hi" and wave when a dark-haired beauty slid out the passenger's side and took his arm. Embarrassed, Lisa ducked her head and quickly got into her own car. What a fool she'd almost made of herself. She'd better learn not to be so impulsive in the future. Embarrassed or not, she couldn't keep her eyes off the good-looking couple making their way inside the restaurant.

It took several seconds for Lisa to recover from her near blunder, and when she had her emotions under control she drove home. In an attempt to ignore the scene she had just witnessed Lisa tried humming along with the radio again, but her singing now sounded flat. Reaching over she turned the music off.

The unexpected sight of the dark-haired female clinging to Grant's arm had shattered her good mood. Repeatedly, she told herself it was none of her concern if Grant was dating such a beautiful woman, but Lisa's cheerful disposition never returned.

Grant's personal life was none of her business, except, of course, in regards to Todd. Now, if he had broken his promise to Todd and hadn't showed up today, that would be another matter all together. She would never stand quietly by and allow her brother to be hurt.

## Chapter Four

Lisa unlocked the door and stepped inside. "I'm home."

Todd dashed from the bedroom. "You'll never guess what happened today."

So, she'd been right, Grant had reneged on his promise. "Grant didn't make it over." Lisa's response was abrupt and unenthusiastic.

"Heck no. What ever gave you that idea?"

Having already found Grant guilty, Lisa wasn't expecting her brother's reply and was completely caught off guard. "I ... it just seemed likely. After all, he is a busy man," she stammered. Lisa hoped Todd didn't question her answer. How could she

49

explain the doubts that had filled her mind upon seeing Grant with his date?

Todd scowled at his sister. "Grant came by early and we had a great day." His voice reflected his impatience with Lisa's suggestion. "We went bowling and then we had lunch. After that we went to the community center and played some basketball."

Lisa gave Todd an apologetic smile, but inwardly she sighed. She had forgotten how much Todd idolized Grant. In the future she'd better be careful of sounding critical of the man. "I'm glad you two had an exciting, fun day," she said, her voice cheerful. She wanted to erase the tension her innocent slip of the tongue had caused.

A slow smile replaced the scowl on Todd's face.

Relieved, Lisa turned and hung up her raincoat in the closet.

"Wait," Todd said. "You haven't heard the exciting part yet."

Lisa faced her brother, but before she could say anything Todd continued. "You got a special delivery package today. The man was walking back to his truck with it when Grant brought me home. The guy drove off before we could stop him, so we chased him down in Grant's car. Of course, if we'd been in a police car with a siren and flashing lights it would have been even more exciting. But Grant said he'd take me for a ride in a patrol car someday."

Lisa rolled her eyes upward. *Think before you speak,* she reminded herself. "I'm glad today wasn't the day for that ride in the police car. I can't imagine what our neighbors would think if the two of you chased down the delivery man with sirens and flashing lights, or how embarrassed the poor delivery man would have been."

"Aw, Sis, where's your sense of humor? It would have been funny. You really do need to lighten up."

"Maybe." Lisa placed her tote bag on the floor of the closet. Grant hadn't disappointed her brother, and for that she was grateful. A brief smile flickered across her face as she pictured Grant and Todd chasing the delivery man. At least they hadn't used a siren and flashing light on the poor guy. Mindful of setting a good example for her brother, Lisa repressed her smile when she turned back to Todd. "Is macaroni and cheese for dinner all right with you?"

Exasperated, Todd shook his head. "Well, aren't you the least bit curious?"

"Curious?"

"Yes. Curious about the package."

"Oh, yes. Let's see what this mysterious package is." Although she tried to be enthusiastic, and she knew she had no right to be envious, Lisa was still reeling from seeing Grant with his date.

Todd hurried to the kitchen, returning with a box and handed it to his sister. Lisa accepted it with forced eagerness. It was a good sized package, about twelve by twenty inches and fifteen inches deep. Her enthusiasm might be forced, but her curiosity was real.

A glance at the initials and return address in the upper left corner of the package confirmed the 'surprise' was from Ralph. Her excitement grew. Ralph was always great about sending her flowers, but this definitely wasn't flowers. Carefully she tore the brown wrapping away, revealing a solid packing box. *Whatever it was, it must be fragile*. Mentally she crossed her fingers, hoping nothing was broken.

Lisa tossed aside the heavy lid only to discover a shoe box cushioned with paper nestled inside the thick cardboard carton. When the final lid was removed her soaring spirits immediately did a nose-dive. What was it? An ugly wooden object rested on a bed of white tissue paper.

Todd interrupted her thoughts. "What is it?"

She wasn't sure, but it was definitely the most frightful looking thing she'd seen in a long time. "I . . . I don't know." Lisa turned it end to end, but even after a thorough examination she was still puzzled. "Oh, here's a note."

*Dear Lisa,*

*How do you like it? I only wish it was the real thing. I found it during a visit to an out-of-the-way antique store. The guy behind the counter tried to pass it off as an authentic statue of an island god, but I knew it was a fake right from the start. When I showed the fellow my credentials he admitted the statue was probably a fraud so he gave me a good deal on it.*

*As I said in my letter I've missed you and think it's time we get serious about our future together. When I came across this statue I decided it would make the perfect engagement gift, even if it is a reproduction.*

*I know you're not as crazy about history and artifacts as I am, but as my wife you'll need to develop a taste and some knowledge of past civilizations. Although this statue isn't genuine it can serve as a springboard of enlightenment.*

*Love, Ralph*

*P.S. Wish I could be there to share this moment with you.*

Todd waited for Lisa to finish reading. "Well, what is it?"

"Ah—it's a statue of some South Sea Island god, I think?"

Todd shook his head. "Boy, he's the ugliest god I've ever seen."

"I agree," Lisa said. "But then, I'm not acquainted with too many gods." She thought about the last two lines of Ralph's note. Maybe she did need to broaden her artistic horizons. "Perhaps with time, old wooden face here will grow on us." Lisa hoped she sounded convincing.

"Don't count on it," Todd replied, turning toward the bedroom.

Just before the bedroom door closed, Lisa was sure she heard the words, "that's the ugliest thing I've ever seen."

She had to agree with Todd, but still she didn't want to hurt Ralph's feelings. But

Lisa couldn't imagine how Ralph thought this ugly thing was going to enrich her life.

Even after a thorough examination Lisa found little about the statue that appealed to her tastes. The statue had bulging muscles and seemed to be standing at attention with a claw of a hand wrapped around an inadequate wisp of a spear. It had a flat triangular head, and its carved face was graced with one enormous eye and was surrounded by colorful zigs and zags of paint. It looked as though it could be as much at home standing on its head as its feet.

To test her theory she stood the creature on its head on the end table. *She was right.* Laughing to herself, she wondered what Ralph would say if he walked in and found his *magnificent* statue doing a head stand in her living room. Retrieving the object, she carefully placed it inside the shoe box. Since she wasn't expecting Ralph home for several weeks she needn't put his *Island god* on display as yet. By the time Ralph returned, maybe she would be more appreciative of his gift.

Usually she wasn't an ungrateful person, but this—this thing was unattractive in addition to being inappropriate. When a woman became engaged, she kind of hoped for a ring, not a one-eyed wooden god to sit on the coffee table. Lisa didn't consider herself a romantic, but surely an engagement gift called for more thought and feeling than Ralph had shown.

Seething with disappointment, Lisa pressed the lid on the shoe box, placing the box on the top shelf of the living room closet. Striding down the hall she knocked on the bedroom door to tell Todd dinner would be ready shortly, thus avoiding his usual pre-dinner snacking.

When Todd opened the door she almost forgot what she wanted when she looked at the mess strewn across the room. "What are you doing?" Lisa inquired.

"Grant helped me find some boxes today and I'm packing for our move. It looks messy now, but by morning I'll have everything in order."

"My, but the two of you were busy today. I'm glad to see you found some boxes. I wasn't as fortunate, but tomorrow I plan on being the earlier bird that catches some boxes."

Todd gave his sister a funny look.

Lisa's eyebrows arched slightly. "Remember, you told me I needed to lighten up. Well, that was a joke. Haven't you ever heard of the early bird who catches the worm?"

"Oh yeah." Todd gave her a condescending smile and rolled his eyes. "I forgot about that old saying."

Lisa frowned. The way Todd emphasized the word old, she felt as though she had aged considerably, and her expression must have revealed her thoughts.

Todd tossed the green turtleneck he held in his hands toward the stack of clothes on the bed. "Sorry if I hurt your feelings. Grant warned me you might be a little touchy."

Lisa's back immediately stiffened. It was one thing for Todd to make her feel ancient, but another thing entirely for Grant to discuss her disposition with her brother. "He said I was touchy?"

Todd quickly tried to amend his blunt statement. "Not exactly. But he did say I needed to be patient with you since you've been living by yourself for so long. He said it takes awhile before a person is completely comfortable sharing their space. And I agree with him," Todd said. "After all, I did suddenly appear on the scene and crowd you out."

Lisa inhaled a deep breath and her frustration slowly ebbed. Perhaps at times she did overreact to things. "I suppose he's right to a degree," she muttered. "But Todd, I want you to know I don't mind sharing anything I have with you."

Todd looked down at the floor as if he was uncomfortable by Lisa's admission. "Ah ... anyway, I'm sorry if I came across as rude."

Unable to control her emotions, Lisa drew Todd near, smothering him in her arms. "I think we both need to show a little more tolerance for one another."

By now Todd was turning crimson color, but he exchanged a smile with Lisa and the strained atmosphere between them evaporated. "I think I'll go fix dinner now," Lisa said.

The first thing Lisa did when she awakened the next morning was check on the weather. Disappointed she closed the drape against the gray murky sky. She hoped the overcast would burn off by afternoon, otherwise they would be moving in the rain.

Dressing quickly in jeans and a T shirt, Lisa gulped down a cup of coffee then drove to the supermarket at the shopping center.

Minutes later she had managed to get six boxes in her car by nesting them, and the store had promised to save her some more.

By the time she and Todd stopped for a lunch break they had most of the boxes packed. "Did Grant say what time he was coming by?" Lisa asked.

Before Todd could speak, however, the telephone rang. Lisa carefully made her way through the maze of boxes scattered about the room, picking the phone up on the third ring.

Recognizing Grant's voice, Lisa chuckled. "My goodness, we must be operating on mental telepathy. I just asked Todd if he knew when you we're coming by."

"I'll be over about five." Grant's words flowed through the wires like warm melted butter causing ripples of pleasure to caress her heart. "We can load my station wagon with the small items and boxes. Tomorrow I'll borrow a friend's truck and we'll move the big stuff. It shouldn't take more than a couple of trips to complete the job." His voice was deep, quiet and comforting. "Does that sound okay with you?"

For a moment Lisa stood there, grinning like a contented cat. "Yes," she purred.

"Good. I'll see you in a little bit."

Grant arrived precisely at five, and before long he and Todd had the station wagon loaded. While they were transporting the first load Lisa emptied her closets. Draping clothes, still on hangers, across the seat of her car, she was ready to follow the guys when they made their second trip.

In spite of their busy night the evening passed quickly amid jokes and good-natured teasing. When the last box was brought in, to Lisa's surprise and Todd's delight, Grant ordered a pizza to be delivered.

"Can I spend the night here?" Todd asked, finishing off the last piece of pizza.

Lisa looked at Todd, her expression full of concern. "Where would you sleep? The bed won't be moved in until tomorrow."

"The floor will do fine. Please, Lisa."

"I don't know. You'll be all alone."

"Grant will be next door." He looked at Grant, his eyes silently begging for support.

"Sure, I'll be next door. If Todd needs anything I'll only be a few steps away." Then, looking at Todd, "You know it really isn't fair for the two of us to gang up on your sister this way."

Lisa was weakening. "Won't you be uncomfortable on the floor?"

"I have a sleeping bag he could use if that would ease your mind," Grant added.

Lisa was ready to concede defeat. "You

won't mind keeping an eye on him?" Her question was directed at Grant.

Todd scowled at his sister, then looked at Grant. His expression clearly said he didn't need looking after. Turning back to Lisa he said, "I'm not a little kid any more. Grant doesn't need to baby sit me."

Grant returned Todd's look with a wink. "Better not push your luck." And to Lisa, "I won't mind."

"Sorry Sis," came Todd's somewhat reluctant reply.

Lisa smiled at the two of them. She was confident Grant would keep a watchful eye on her brother whether Todd wanted it or not. "All right, you can spend the night, but don't stay up all evening."

She gave her brother a hug. "I might as well be going. There doesn't appear to be anything else I can do here. See you in the morning."

Moving alongside Lisa, Grant gently placed his hand on her elbow. "I'm going to walk your sister to her car. I'll be right back." And as they got out of ear-shot of Todd, "I just wanted to reassure you. Todd will be fine. He talks big. All kids his age do. But if he changes his mind about staying alone in the duplex tonight he can come stay with me."

Lisa smiled her thanks to Grant. "I know I can count on you to keep an eye on Todd." But as she continued to look into Grant's face her thoughts turned from her brother to the uneven beat of her heart. There was no denying the fact that she was attracted to Grant.

The sky had already taken on a blue-black silkiness, and there was only a slice of moon in the sky so Lisa was unable to clearly make out Grant's features, but she was very much aware of the man who stood inches away from her. The faint scent of his after shave, which had a citrus smell, was as intoxicating as a fine wine. And his gaze transcended the darkness immobilizing her body and her brain. This was definitely not what she wanted. Somehow she found the strength to step back. The movement worked to clear her mind. Grant was not right for her. She needed someone safe.

Frightened by the depth of her emotions, Lisa turned quickly for the safety of her car, but Grant caught her hand. The warmth of his touch was like a hot ember against her skin. With a muffled 'oh' she pulled her hand free and slid behind the steering wheel.

When Grant leaned down to the opened window Lisa's heart began pounding so hard she thought it might jump completely out of her chest. "Thanks for your help," she murmured, then started the car.

"Todd and I will be by early, so don't sleep in," Grant said as she drove away. Even without looking, Lisa knew there was a grin on his face.

By the time she arrived back at her old apartment, her heartbeat had returned to normal, but her confusion had not subsided.

Already in a muddled state, Lisa was overwhelmed with a sense of dejection when she entered the small living room. The nearly empty apartment echoed with loneliness. Without Todd's presence the place seemed lifeless. It was funny, but what she missed was the noise and turbulence that seemed to be Todd's natural aura. She smiled to herself. She'd better not let Todd know she was becoming such a mother-hen.

After a quick shower Lisa retired to the bedroom and for the first time since Todd's arrival she stretched out in her own bed. It felt so good she couldn't resist a sigh as the tightness seemed to dissolve from her muscles. She did not look forward to sleeping on the sofa again. Friday, after work she would see about getting Todd a new bedroom set. Now that they would each have their own room there was no reason to delay.

Adjusting her pillow she turned onto her side expecting to drift off immediately. But thirty minutes later, unable to put aside her earlier encounter with Grant, Lisa found herself wide awake. She kept wondering what it would have been like if they had kissed. She was sure he had wanted to kiss her. Why had she fled like a scared rabbit? She knew the answer of course. She was afraid to fall for someone like Grant. Her future was much more secure with Ralph.

The thought of Ralph jolted Lisa from her dreamy thoughts of Grant. According to Ralph's note she was an engaged woman now. But a small voice quickly suppressed that idea. After all, she hadn't said yes— had she?

Grabbing her pillow and hugging it close, she counted sheep. At number ninety-nine she fell asleep.

## Chapter Five

Despite the problem she'd had falling asleep, Lisa was dressed and at the small market on the corner by seven the next morning.

When Grant and Todd arrived at the duplex an hour later, she had coffee and doughnuts waiting for them.

By noon the three of them had everything moved and unloaded. "I hate to leave you with such a mess," Grant apologized, "but I've got some paperwork at the office that I need to finish before five o'clock." His expression was sympathetic.

Not allowing him to continue, Lisa raised her hand in attempt to ward off further apologies. "Please, you've done enough as it is. Todd and I can handle the rest."

His eyes brightened. "All right. I'll see you later this evening."

Lisa followed Grant to the door. "Thanks for your help."

For a moment he stood looking at her, saying nothing. Lisa could feel that warm glow begin in the pit of her stomach again. In that instant she had the strangest desire to reach out and touch Grant. It was almost a need more than a desire. Over the last few days his friendship had become special to her and the fear that he might not return suddenly enveloped her. To hide her emotions she broke eye contact with him. "See you later," she whispered.

Grant moved toward her ever so slightly then stopped. "You can count on it neighbor." Then he was gone.

Her emotions tumbling as if caught in a wind storm, Lisa closed the door. For awhile she stood facing the door while trying to compose herself. Taking a deep breath and having control of her feelings, Lisa turned to Todd.

Her composure quickly disappeared, however, when she surveyed the chaos scattered about the living room. She was in no mood to unpack. What she needed was a change of scenery. "Todd, I don't suppose you'd be interested in going shopping for a bedroom set?"

Todd looked at Lisa, a perplexed expression on his face. "Right now?"

Lisa smiled. "Right now."

Todd set down the box he was holding. "You don't have to ask me twice. I'm ready when you are."

An hour later, Todd had picked out a rustic wooden bedroom set that included a dresser and night stand. After purchasing bed linens and a mattress, Lisa had spent a considerable amount, but the gratitude on Todd's face assured her it was worth it. And when she thought of how great it would feel to have her own bed to herself again she knew the money was well spent.

Todd gave his sister an appreciative look. "I really feel like my stay with you is permanent now."

"Silly, of course it's permanent. We're family and we're going to be together at least until you graduate from high school." Lisa laid her arm across her brother's shoulder and hugged him. She hadn't realized how deep his insecurities went.

Todd, a typical thirteen-year-old, pulled

away and glanced around as if he was afraid someone had seen them. "Not here, Lisa."

Lisa restrained the smile that threatened to spring forth upon her lips. There were no other teenagers in the furniture department, but she certainly didn't want to embarrass Todd, even accidently. "Sorry, I forgot we're in a public place."

"That's okay, Sis."

Lisa cleared her throat. "You know Grant has been a big help to us." Todd nodded his head in agreement. "And I'd like to get him something to show our appreciation. Got any suggestions?"

"How about a big pepperoni pizza?" Todd teased, his eyes bright with humor.

"Sure." Lisa said, giving him a rap on the arm. "And you'd eat half of it. Anyway this is a department store, not a pizzeria. Come on now, get serious."

"Cologne?"

"Not cologne, that's too personal. I was thinking more like something for his house."

"Gripes, you're not thinking about getting him one of those ugly statues, are you?"

Lisa tried giving Todd a stern look, but she couldn't be mad at him. Besides, the thought of Grant unwrapping a package and finding the funny little wooden statue caused her to laugh in spite of herself. "No. I doubt he'd appreciate a statue like that."

"Thank goodness. I wouldn't want him to kick us out before my new furniture arrives."

Lisa chuckled. "I don't think you need to worry. You and Grant seem to be getting along just fine." She stopped in front of a display of clocks, picking up a copper wall clock with Roman numerals. Turning it over, she examined it front and back. The clock looked like something a man might buy. She wondered if Grant would like a new clock. After a few seconds she set it back. Somehow a clock didn't seem right either.

Todd tugged at the sleeve of Lisa's jacket. "Don't get him that, Sis. I know exactly what he'd like. Follow me."

"Where are we going?"

"Wait until we get there."

Lisa trailed behind Todd, following him to the electronic section of the department store. What did Todd have in mind? A radio? A record?

"Here we are, and before you say no, I know he wants this."

Wants what? Lisa stood before a glass

case filled with small colorful boxes. She really didn't know what she was suppose to be looking for. "Ah . . . Todd, you're going to have to tell me what it is he wants."

"A computer game." Todd's patience was wearing thin. "He wants a new game called Neighborhood Bully."

"You've got be kidding?" Lisa was sure her mouth must have fallen open with surprise.

Although she wasn't into video and computer games, she knew they were popular with the younger set. But with grown men? She wasn't certain about Todd's suggestion and didn't want to insult Grant. "You're positive he likes video games?"

Todd gave her a sheepish look. "Well, when we were at the bowling alley, we only bowled one game. Most of the time we played the video machines."

She should have known. Wasn't Grant the same man who flew a model plane around the school yard? She didn't think she needed to worry about insulting him. "If I buy this game, how do I know he has a computer to play it on?"

Todd looked at Lisa. His innocent look changed abruptly to an impish grin. "Because last night we went to Grant's and played computer games."

"I see." Still she wasn't sure a computer game was what she wanted to buy. Her uncertainty must have registered on her face.

"Trust me, it's what he wants," Todd encouraged, pointing out the game disc that was compatible with Grant's computer.

Lisa still had her doubts as she walked away clutching the small package, but the salesman behind the counter had assured her *grown men* did use their computers for more than work. In fact, the look he gave her suggested she must have been asleep for the last ten years. Living with Todd was going to be a real eye opener—she could tell.

On the way home Lisa stopped at the supermarket. Still apprehensive about the appropriateness of a computer game, she planned on inviting Grant to dinner as an additional way of saying thanks. "I won't be long," she promised Todd as she got out of the car and hurried toward the store.

Twenty minutes later Lisa had a big pot of spaghetti sauce simmering on the kitchen stove. Then procuring Todd's help the two of them tackled the disarray in the living and dining rooms.

"Boy, that sure smells good," Todd commented as the spicy aroma wafted into where they were working.

A glimmer of humor crossed Lisa's face. "Let's hope Grant doesn't have plans for dinner, and that he likes spaghetti. Otherwise we'll be eating leftover spaghetti for days." Her comment was made in jest, but Lisa truly hoped Grant didn't have other plans and not just because they'd be dining on spaghetti for a week.

Working together it didn't take Lisa and Todd long to have the visible areas of the duplex presentable. Their bedrooms, however, bulged with stuff that would have to be dealt with at a later time. But for tonight Lisa did not want to worry about it.

Lisa pushed a small box into the coat closet. Standing up, she wiped her brow. "That's enough for now. Don't you agree?"

Todd nodded, shoving the stack of books he was holding into the closet, next to the box Lisa had placed there.

Refreshed from a quick shower, Lisa emerged from her bedroom in a clean pair of tan trousers and a blue and tan striped top just as a car pulled into the driveway. Lisa glanced at her watch. It was only ten minutes to five. Grant must have finished a wee bit earlier than expected.

In the living room, she paused for a last look in the mirror above the phone stand. Satisfied with what she saw Lisa stepped to the window. Her hopes fell when she saw the small yellow car parked on Grant's side of the driveway. Puzzled, Lisa watched as the driver's door opened and the raven-haired beauty stepped out. Lisa winced, moving back from the window.

Disappointed, she bit her lip. Grant must be more serious about this woman than Lisa realized. "So be it!" she mumbled to herself. Straightening her shoulders, she swallowed her disappointment and walked to the kitchen. She knew Grant had a girlfriend. So why was she feeling so depressed? Lisa meant nothing to Grant. She was only his neighbor and he was her landlord. In the future she'd do well to remember that.

Lisa picked up the blue and white pot holder from the counter and lifted the lid to the spaghetti sauce. She stirred the tomato concoction and dropped the lid back on the pot. It didn't look as though Grant would be joining them for dinner. Maybe she'd freeze some of the sauce, that is if she could find some containers. Her search for containers was interrupted by the ringing of the doorbell. She jerked in reaction to the bell, almost bumping her head on the counter.

That was probably Grant, and at the moment she wasn't sure she could face him, but she couldn't leave him out on the porch ringing the doorbell. Hoping her face didn't reveal her inner feelings, Lisa slowly walked to the living room, but to her relief Todd passed her like a speeding bullet.

"That's probably Grant," he said over his shoulder.

Happy to let Todd answer the door, Lisa moved back to the dining room where she was partially hidden by a hanging plant.

*What nerve.* Grant and the beauty queen stood on her doorstep. Afraid emotions she couldn't control might surface, she took another step back, hoping Todd could handle whatever Grant wanted. But Todd, unaware of her feelings, invited them inside. "Come here, Lisa," Todd called to his sister.

Since she couldn't very well pretend she hadn't heard him, Lisa swallowed her resentment and walked forward. *Keep your cool.* Don't let on you're upset, she told herself, as she came face to face with Grant's date.

Lisa did a quick appraisal. The woman was about her age, and tall, but that was probably all they had in common. Her rich ebony hair waved about her shoulders and her dark eyes glowed with a spirited independence. She seemed perfect.

Lisa's left hand went up and she fingered her own brown locks, pulled back with a ribbon. She should have taken more time with her appearance, not that it mattered, but still . . .

The woman gave Lisa a warm friendly smile which only made her feel worse. Under different circumstances Lisa would have probably liked this dark-haired woman.

Lisa returned the woman's smile, then looked at Grant. "It's very nice of you to stop by, but please, we don't expect you to interrupt your social life for us. Everything is under control."

Grant's look was one of puzzlement. "You're not interrupting my plans. If anything I'm probably the one who's interrupting you, but I wanted you to meet my sister, Beth. She lives and works in Seattle, and has to drive back in the morning to start another modeling job."

*Sister*? The smile Lisa gave Beth wasn't the least bit forced this time. "I'm so pleased to meet you," her words came rushing out.

"The feeling is mutual. Grant's been telling me all about his new neighbors and I'm glad I had the chance to meet you before I leave town."

Grant cleared his throat. "I was going to take Beth to dinner. Would you and Todd like to join us?"

"I have a better idea. I've got a big pot of spaghetti cooking on the stove. Why don't you and Beth have dinner with us instead."

"Come on, say yes," Todd begged.

"After moving today, you must be tired. Are you sure you feel like fixing dinner?"

"It's already prepared. Besides, you'll be doing us a big favor," Lisa added. "Otherwise, we're going to be eating spaghetti for a long time."

"If it's okay with Beth, it's okay with me."

Beth flashed Grant an approving smile. "Sounds good to me. Why don't you sit yourself down, while I see if there's anything I can help Lisa with in the kitchen."

"There really isn't much to do, but follow me," Lisa said turning towards the kitchen. "I'd love the company."

Fifteen minutes later they called the guys to dinner.

"You know Grant, you're very lucky to have a neighbor who cooks," Beth teased her brother. "Maybe you should offer her a discount on her rent for a free meal now and then."

Grant gave his sister an indignant frown. The others could tell it was all in fun, however. "You're being a little harsh. I can cook."

"Sure-sure, you can broil a steak, fry an egg, and make coffee. And your coffee's a little strong at that."

"That's the way I like it, little sister."

So they had something else in common, Lisa mused. She couldn't start her day without a potent cup of coffee.

Todd's voice broke into her thoughts. "Shall we give Grant his present?"

Todd's question caught her off guard and Lisa felt an embarrassing flush as the others fixed their gaze on her. For fear of appearing too forward, Lisa hastily explained to Beth. "It's just a small gift. You know— for all the help your brother has given us."

Todd jumped up from his chair. "I'll go get it." Seconds later, he stood in front of Grant with the small wrapped package.

"It isn't much," Lisa said, in a soft voice. "But Todd assured me this was what you would like."

Grant's face broke into a wide little-boy grin. "Do you know how long it's been since

someone has surprised me with a present?"
His voice pealed with excitement. Todd
handed Grant the gaily wrapped packaged
and he wasted no time tearing the paper
away. Astonishment and delight played
across his face when he saw the computer
game. "This is exactly what I've been want-
ing. How did you know?"

Lisa, unaware she'd been holding her
breath, exhaled and looked at her brother.
"Todd picked it out. He said it was what you
wanted."

"Looks like your new neighbors know you
pretty well big brother," Beth quipped.
"That gleam in your eye tells me you can't
wait to try it out, so why don't you and Todd
load it into your computer, while I help Lisa
with the dishes."

Todd and Grant acted promptly on Beth's
suggestion and headed for Grant's apartment with the game disc.

"That should keep them busy for the rest
of the evening," Beth said, helping Lisa
clear the table.

As they worked over the dishes the two
women became better acquainted. Lisa soon
realized a strong sense of love and loyalty
existed between Beth and Grant.

"I'm so glad you and Todd have moved

next door to my brother," Beth said matter-of-factly. "Grant may be older than me, but I still can't help worrying about him. He's all the family I've got and I'd like to see him settled down and happy."

Lisa swallowed. Did Beth think there was a chance for more than friendship between Grant and herself? She had to admit she found him appealing. But then, there was the matter of his job. Memories of the night the Fire Chief knocked on the Bowmans' door flashed through Lisa's mind. The pain and grief of that evening rushed in upon her. No, she simply couldn't handle Grant's job. But, if he was willing to change jobs— Lisa wondered if he would consider such a move?

Beth's next words dashed that idea. "Did you know that Grant is divorced? Melody, his ex-wife, didn't like being married to a policeman. She was constantly harping at him to quit and go into the realty business with her father, but Grant refused. Then when Melody filed for divorce he almost gave in to her demands, but at the last minute he changed his mind. He's wanted to be a policeman since he was a kid."

"Oh," Lisa managed through dry lips.

Beth smiled at her. "Anyway, Grant needs someone who can accept him and make him happy. Like he was tonight," she added none too subtly.

## Chapter Six

Lisa stood on the front stoop, her shoulder gently brushing Grant's, and watched as Beth backed the yellow car from the driveway. The accidental contact sent a delightful shiver down her arm, but she purposely ignored it. Beth's words rang like a warning in her head. Grant had been hurt once before by a woman who couldn't accept his lifestyle, Lisa didn't want to add to his pain. Like his ex-wife, she knew she could not tolerate his work.

Grant turned to Lisa as the yellow car disappeared around the corner. "Well, what did you think of Beth?"

"She's beautiful, and I think she cares

about her big brother very much. You're lucky to have such a doting sister."

"Ah-yes. My doting sister. She didn't by any chance try to play matchmaker while the two of you were alone? I think it's her mission in life to see me married again. I assume she told you I was divorced?"

"Why, yes. She did."

"Is that one yes or two?"

"Two," Lisa whispered, feeling a little embarrassed at the turn of their conversation.

Grant stared down at her, his gaze locked with hers, draining her of her will to resist. When he moved closer Lisa didn't back away. She knew he was going to kiss her and she tilted her head to meet his mouth. His lips were warm and gentle as they caressed her own, but too quickly he pulled away.

"What my sister doesn't seem to understand—I believe in taking my time. I don't need her help. I'll know when I'm falling in love."

Choked with emotion, Lisa swallowed, unable to think of a response.

Tenderly, Grant cupped her chin in his palm and ever so lightly brushed his lips against hers. "Good night neighbor."

Lisa stood on the porch watching as Grant

entered his own unit. The tingling she felt finally reached her toes. She hated to move—to break the spell, but she knew if she stood there much longer Todd would come looking for her.

When she retired to her room Lisa scolded herself for letting a couple of kisses overrule her common sense. She should not be encouraging Grant. Which meant, of course, that she should not be encouraging his kisses either.

She knew by the way Grant was looking at her that he was going to kiss her, and she should have resisted—even a little. But she had wanted his kiss and she had been too weak to turn away. Lisa smiled to herself. She hadn't been disappointed. Grant's kiss had turned out to be everything she had imagined it to be. But in the future there'd be no more kisses, only memories, she promised herself.

Throwing back the covers, Lisa crawled into bed and closed her eyes. Her dreams that night were filled with visions of her neighbor.

Friday was another gray, overcast day, but Lisa was certain the haze would burn off by the afternoon. But even if it didn't, at least moving was behind her. Grabbing her book bag she headed for work.

She had been right, Lisa mused, as she pulled her old Chevy into the driveway of the duplex later that afternoon. The sun now blinked down from above filling the car's interior with its lulling rays. She shut off the ignition, and like a preening cat stretched, trying to ward off the drowsiness that threatened to overtake her. The job of moving had taken more out of her than she realized.

Stifling a yawn, she opened the door to the duplex. Todd was nowhere about, but she found a note posted to the mirror over the phone stand.

*Lisa, I met the kid across the street today, and we went down to the recreational center. My furniture was delivered and set up, too. Todd*

When Lisa entered Todd's room she was pleased to see that without any nagging from her, he had made his bed. She must remember to thank him. Already she was seeing a change in Todd's attitude.

After checking out the new furniture,

Lisa decided to take advantage of the quiet and reclined on the sofa.

A couple of hours later Todd gently shook her shoulder, waking her from her pleasant nap. "Hey, Sis. Did you see my room?"

Lisa awakened with a start. "Room?" Still drowsy she shook her head in an effort to cast off the remnants of sleep. "Oh, yes. Your room looks nice, and I was pleased to see you got your bed together by yourself."

"Grant says a guy should know how to take care of things around the house. It's good practice for when you get a place of your own," Todd informed his sister.

Lisa had to repress the smile on her lips. "I couldn't agree more. Now, what would you like for dinner, sandwiches or left over spaghetti?"

Before Todd could state his preference the doorbell rang. The next thing Lisa knew Todd had opened the door and Grant had entered the room.

Lisa gave him a feeble smile. *Why did he always catch her at her worst.* She might not be Sleeping Beauty, and Grant certainly wasn't *her* prince charming, but as a female she was just vain enough to want to make a respectable appearance. "Hi."

"Rough day?" Grant's voice was gentle and caring.

Lisa pushed herself up off the sofa. "Not really. The afternoon sun just brought out a lazy streak."

Grant laughed. "Good. I'm glad to hear it's nothing serious, because I've got some free tickets for the Tigers baseball game tonight. I thought you and Todd might like to go."

Todd's enthusiastic "yes," and questions about who they were playing gave Lisa time to think. She liked baseball, and it would be fun, but she couldn't possibly accept his invitation. If anything, she needed to put some distance between herself and Grant. It was time to start thinking with her head instead of her heart. "Thanks for asking, but I really need to stay home and finish unpacking tonight."

A trace of disappointment flashed across Grant's face. He recovered quickly, but she had seen it. In that instant Lisa was certain she was doing the right thing—they must not become romantically involved. They would both end up being hurt.

A groan to her left drew Lisa's attention. "Gosh, Sis, I thought we were just about done with the unpacking."

Lisa looked at her brother whose expression was a mixture of pain and anger. Understanding dawned. *Todd thinks he can't go if I don't go.* She quickly reassured him. "You don't have to stay home just because I do. The two of you can still go."

Todd immediately relaxed.

"Are you positive we can't talk you into going?" Grant asked. "The ball game is sure to be more fun than unpacking."

Lisa looked into his eyes and found herself weakening. It was as though his innermost thoughts were mirrored in their gold-flecked depths. He sincerely wanted her to go, she could tell.

Afraid her own eyes would give her away, Lisa turned from Grant to Todd. "Maybe next time."

"All right. I'll let you off the hook, but I won't be so easy on you next time." Grant winked. Then he looked over at Todd. "Come on over to my place in about thirty minutes."

When Grant left, Lisa rose. "I guess we'd better have sandwiches if you're going to a game in thirty minutes."

Lisa removed two boxes from her bedroom closet. Todd was right, there wasn't much that needed to be unpacked. The first box contained odds and ends, most of which should have probably gone out with the rest of the stuff she'd donated to the second hand store. The second box was filled with books and some knickknacks. Oh well, if she finished early she'd watch TV.

Lisa poked through the box of books and soon found herself completely absorbed. Todd wasn't much on reading but maybe she could get him interested in Jack London's *Call of the Wild*, or in *All Creatures Great and Small*: they were both good reading.

She had just placed the last of the books in the oak bookcase when the telephone rang. Glad for the interruption, Lisa picked up the receiver, hoping it wasn't a wrong number.

"Hello."

"So, I finally caught you home."

Lisa recognized the voice. "Ralph, what a pleasant surprise."

Ignoring Lisa's enthusiastic greeting, Ralph continued his lecture. "I've had a devil of a time trying to get you. Have you gotten yourself talked into another project? I know you find it difficult to turn anyone down. But you must learn to say No." He sharply emphasized the no.

Lisa sighed. At times Ralph just didn't understand. He thought she allowed herself to be manipulated into volunteering too much. Like her work at the Inner-City Community Church. Nobody had forced her, she just wanted to do it. "No, Ralph, I haven't taken on any new projects, unless you want to consider moving a new project."

"You moved? But you've got the same phone number."

"We didn't move that far away. We're still in the same prefix area. That's why the phone number didn't change."

"I see." He paused for a minute. "Since you moved, does that mean you didn't get my letter and package?"

"They both arrived before we moved. You should be getting my letter any day now," Lisa said.

"And . . ."

"And I'll be glad to meet your plane."

"That's not exactly what I was talking about," Ralph answered a little crisply.

Lisa knew what he was waiting to hear, why was she so reluctant to commit herself. *Ralph would make her a perfect husband.* The next few words tumbled out of her mouth before she could stop them. "I'm just a bit disappointed. Perhaps I'm a little old fashioned, but I believe in the traditional engagement ring."

"You don't like the statue?" Ralph sounded genuinely surprised.

"I like it fine," Lisa said, crossing her fingers.

There was a long sigh on the other end of the line. "That's a relief. I can't imagine marrying someone who doesn't appreciate the arts."

Lisa took a deep breath. "Ralph, the statue is okay, but when a girl becomes engaged she wants a ring."

"All right my old fashioned lady. If you want a ring, I'll get a ring. But let me warn you—in the future I won't be so easy to twist around your finger." His words were punctuated with a short laugh, but there was little humor in his voice.

"Thanks for understanding, Ralph. And you needn't worry—I don't see you as a man who can be twisted around anyone's finger."

Lisa's declaration seemed to ease the tension surrounding their conversation. "That's one of the things I like about you, Lisa. You're very perceptive."

"And you're very gracious," she whispered softly into the phone.

"Ah—about the statue," Ralph proclaimed. "Did you place it where it's catching some light? It really needs to be spotlighted to be shown at its best." He then went on to give her a little history about the real god whom the statue was suppose to represent.

Lisa could hear the animation in his voice as he discussed the statue. "I'll check on it," she promised. Suddenly a disturbing thought crossed her mind. She hadn't seen the darn thing since moving. Her stomach knotted in a tight ball.

Fearing she had lost Ralph's precious statue her mind wandered. Where could it be?

"Lisa!"

She quickly jerked to attention at the commanding sound of Ralph's voice. "Are you going to meet my plane?"

"Yes-yes. I promise to be there."

"Good. You know I've missed you a lot. I'm looking forward to our marriage. We'll start planning the wedding as soon as I return."

Lisa responded appropriately and hung up the phone. Her head was pulsing with the beginning of a headache. Where could that statue be?

\* \* \*

Although her eyes were closed, Lisa was not asleep when she heard Grant's car pull into the drive at eleven-thirty. Like a worried mother hen, she could not sleep until her chick—in this case, Todd—was safely accounted for.

Todd's voice floated out on the night air and in through the screened window, reaching Lisa as she lay on the sofa. "Thanks Grant, for the ball game and pizza."

"Sure thing," came the deep masculine reply.

Their voices were drowned out for a minute by a plane passing overhead, but Lisa caught the words, "Fourth of July, and I won't say anything."

Grant responded to Todd's statement by saying, "I'll call Lisa tomorrow."

*What were the two of them up to?* Lisa could envision the twinkle in Grant's eyes and the pleased grin on her brother's face.

Still wearing her jeans and T-shirt, Lisa pushed herself up into a sitting position, swinging her feet to the floor. Maybe Todd would let her in on what was going on?

Todd's key sounded in the lock, and her brother stepped into the room. "Oh, hi Sis. Did I wake you?"

"No, I wasn't asleep."

"The ball game was great," Todd said, taking off the baseball cap he was wearing. He held it out for Lisa to see. "Grant bought me this Tiger's cap, too. And the Tigers won, 7–4, but then I knew they'd win. Then on the way home we stopped for pizza. It wasn't just a one-topping pizza, either. We ordered the deluxe. Too bad you didn't go. You sure missed out on a good time."

The corners of Lisa's mouth twitched with a smile. "Listening to you, I can tell that I missed out. Maybe I'll get another chance one of these days. But let me warn you, I don't want anchovies on my pizza."

Todd's eyes flashed with humor. "That's the only thing we didn't have on it. And on the Fourth—Oops!" Todd slapped a hand over his mouth then removed it. "I wasn't suppose to say anything," he whispered. The humor in his eyes was replaced with regret over his slip of the tongue.

"Oh?" Lisa said, her mouth curving into a faint smile. "Just what is it you're not suppose to talk about and why?"

Todd's loyalties were obviously divided. Lisa could tell he was having a hard time making his decision.

When he finally spoke, she guessed he decided his duty lay with her.

"We're going to have a barbecue for the Fourth of July. It was suppose to be a surprise. Grant's going to call you tomorrow. Please don't let on you know."

Lisa smiled at her brother. *So that was it.* "I'll pretend to be caught completely off guard," she assured him.

"And you won't say no?" Todd asked.

Lisa hedged. "I didn't agree to that."

"What's the matter, Lisa, don't you like Grant?"

Lisa stood speechless for a second as she considered Todd's question. How could she explain her feelings to him? Todd was too young to understand. He didn't remember those first few years following their father's death and how their mother had changed from a lively person into a sad old lady. Sidestepping the truth, Lisa said, "I like Grant, honey, but I don't want to take advantage of him. He must have other things to do than spend all his time with us."

Todd looked a little bewildered. "But the barbecue was Grant's idea. I'm sure he wouldn't have suggested it if he had other things to do. We're even planning on having our own fireworks show after dinner. Come on, Sis, say it's okay."

Lisa didn't want to say yes, but once again

she found herself in the position of being the *bad guy* if she said no. Surely no harm could come from sharing an outdoor barbecue with Grant, she rationalized.

## Chapter Seven

Lisa was still in bed the next morning when Grant's station wagon rumbled to life as he prepared to leave for work.

Comfortable, she rolled over in bed and smiled. After giving the matter considerable thought, she had decided to accept Grant's invitation for the Fourth. Not only that, she was actually looking forward to it. It sounded like fun. Besides, they were neighbors, and there was no reason they shouldn't share a friendly barbecue together.

At ten o'clock Grant called. "A barbecue sounds like fun," Lisa said into the receiver.

"You mean you're not going to come up

with an excuse?" Grant asked, clearly surprised by her answer.

Her laughter bubbled forth. "No excuses. I'm looking forward to it. I haven't had a barbecue since I was a kid."

"Well then, I guess we'll have to make this barbecue something you'll remember. We'll put on a fantastic Fourth of July display just for you."

"Is that a good idea?"

Deep rich laughter greeted Lisa's ear. "Don't worry, we'll use legal fireworks. They'll still make for a nice show. But I'm glad to see I did make an impression on you that day," he teased.

Lisa smiled as she spoke into the phone. "Let's just say I haven't been lectured so strongly since third grade when Mrs. Wheaton caught me prying the lid off my glue jar with a pair of sharp scissors."

"Good for Mrs. Wheaton. There's a right way and a wrong way to do things. But rest assured we'll follow the rules when we set off our fireworks."

"Then I'll be looking forward to the Fourth," Lisa said.

"Listen, I'm going to be busy working on a case for the next few days so I might not see much of you or Todd, but I'll be home on the Fourth for our barbecue."

"Since you're going to be busy, I'll do the grocery shopping," Lisa said, "and help with dinner."

"I won't argue with that," Grant replied, "but I'll buy the steaks."

Lisa was smiling when she hung up the phone and walked to the kitchen. Todd was sitting at the table eating a bowl of cereal. "Everything is set for the Fourth," she informed him.

His smile went ear to ear. "Good."

She had obviously made his day. Now, if he would help her.

"When you finish your breakfast I need your help," Lisa said in her most beseeching voice.

"What's up?" Todd asked, filling his bowl with a second helping of frosted flakes.

"Remember that package I got the other day?"

"Oh, you mean the one that contained that weird statue?"

"That's the one. Have you seen it?"

"The package or the statue?"

"Either," she said, slightly exasperated.

"No."

Lisa tried to remain calm and composed.

*After all, it wasn't Todd's fault the statue was missing.* Still, her voice reflected her desperation. "Please, try to remember."

Todd reached across the table and picked up a fat flake that had escaped his bowl. "Gosh, Sis, I really haven't seen that package since you opened it." He popped the cereal flake into his mouth. "Once was enough."

Lisa pretended she hadn't heard his remark. "Will you help me look for it, please? It seems to be misplaced."

"Sure."

After an hour of searching, the package was still missing, and the only place they hadn't looked was the garage.

Lisa pressed her fingers to her temples and groaned. She must not panic. But what was she going to do if she couldn't find it? Ralph would surely give her a lecture on responsibility and appreciation, and she'd have to agree with him. Just because she didn't like the statue, she didn't have to lose it.

Todd's voice interrupted her self-reproach. "Well?" He stood there, hands on his hips, a hurry-up and let's get it over with look on his face. "Do we look in the garage?"

She shook her head. She'd already taken

enough of his time. "I know you're anxious to go shoot some baskets, so I'll finish the garage."

"Okay. I'm going over to Steve's house if you want me." Todd quickly retreated down the drive.

"Thanks for your help," Lisa called, unlocking the garage. The door rolled upwards on its tracks with a creaking sound as if warning her she was wasting her time. *Stop it!* she ordered. Her nerves were getting the best of her.

After being outside in the bright sun the interior of the garage appeared to be one big shadow. Blinking, she reached for the light switch. Illumination spilled forth, but after a cursory glance Lisa knew she was wasting her time. There was no shoe box anywhere.

Ready to call a halt to her search she was just about to turn out the light when she spied a carton tucked against the back wall.

Lisa crossed her fingers and walked towards the cardboard box. This had to be it! When she couldn't find the statue, she looked again. How could it not be here? There simply was no place else to look. Reluctant to believe her eyes, she looked again, but no, the box contained papers and mementos from her college and high school days.

Tired and discouraged, Lisa turned off the light and went back inside the duplex, where she collapsed into a weary heap on the sofa. Her head was throbbing with tension.

How could the thing just disappear? It couldn't simply get up and walk away unless the statue had some magical power Ralph had forgotten to tell her about.

Suddenly something clicked in her mind. Of course it didn't get up and walk away, but maybe she had given it away. Because they were moving, she had donated some things to a second hand store. Perhaps the statue had accidently been mixed in with these things?

As much as she wanted to find the statue, at the moment her head was pounding and she was too exhausted to follow up on her idea. What she wanted right now was a long hot bath and a couple of aspirins for her head, but tomorrow she would go to the second hand store.

Now that she knew where the statue was Lisa relaxed somewhat. The statue was so ugly she was sure no one would want to buy it. Of course, she wouldn't be off the hook until she had the thing in her hand, but she felt certain that by this time tomorrow the statue would be back home.

A clerk at the thrift store pointed out the manager to Lisa. He was a big man, dressed in jeans and a rumpled T-shirt, and he looked as though he seldom smiled.

"I'm afraid he's not in a very good mood today," the clerk said. "One of the drivers didn't come in and Stan has had to take his place picking up donations."

*Great.* Taking a deep breath, Lisa drew forth her biggest smile and approached the stern looking manager. She explained her problem as briefly as possible. Lisa knew instinctively she wasn't going to like Stan's answer when he took so much time mulling over her question.

Stan's round puffy face was a mask of indifference when he spoke. "I'm sorry Miss, but I can't help you. I haven't seen the statue you're describing. And even if I had it, I couldn't give it back without the proper authorization."

His words destroyed Lisa's last bit of hope. "Do you mind if I ask some of your employees if they've seen it?"

"Not at all. But you realize, don't you,

that if you find it we can't simply hand it over? We'll have to check the value of the item you want back, and then the owners will have to agree to its return."

Lisa gritted her teeth. "If you've got it, I'll buy the thing back."

The manager nodded and turned. At least he was wearing a smile, Lisa thought, watching him walk away.

Lisa went from employee to employee. They were all friendlier and more sympathetic than the manager, but no one remembered seeing her missing statue.

As a last measure she spent the next twenty minutes browsing through an assortment of odds and ends, some of which looked as ugly and useless as her statue. Her hopes died. Nothing. Dropping the set of hand-painted coasters back in the bin, Lisa was ready to admit her statue wasn't in the store.

After leaving her name and phone number with a clerk, she called it a day. On her way home, she considered her choices. She could tell Ralph the truth and take her lumps, or—perhaps she could find another statue to replace the lost one. She knew her chances of finding the exact statue were slim, but it was worth a try. Ralph wouldn't be home for another two weeks.

Lisa felt wretched the next morning when her alarm went off. Her sleep had been intertwined with two puzzling dreams. In one, Ralph would hand her a shoe box from a never dwindling pile, and of course each box contained a statue with a triangle-shaped head. Even though she was awake the words, "Maybe you won't lose this one," rang in her ears.

The other dream had been even more disturbing. Grant was in a police car chasing a bank robber who was shooting at him. And, although the flying bullets kept missing him, they never ceased.

Unfortunately her day didn't improve. She had visited so many second hand stores she couldn't count them on her fingers, and she still hadn't found what she was looking for. Lisa walked slowly back to her car.

It appeared as though she'd have to settle for her *lumps*. Not that Ralph was going to physically hit her. Heavens no. He wasn't that kind of man, but he was always quick to point out the shortcomings of others, and he surely wouldn't let this incident slide by without making a few choice comments.

The telephone was ringing when Lisa opened the door of the duplex. Grumbling, she hurried across the room and lifted the receiver.

"Hello." Lisa stepped out of her shoes as she waited for a response.

"May I speak to Lisa Bowman?"

The voice sounded familiar, but she couldn't place it. "This is Lisa. May I help you?"

"This is Kay Hammon, Lisa. I was your landlord over on A Street."

"Oh, yes, Mrs. Hammon. I didn't recognize your voice. What can I do for you?"

"Well, I think perhaps I can do something for you. I was cleaning out the duplex today, getting ready to paint . . ."

Whatever it was Mrs. Hammon had to say to her, Lisa knew she would have to listen to a lot of unnecessary chatter before Kay got around to telling her the crux of her story. Kay was a talker and couldn't be rushed.

"I bought this paint on sale—got a good deal on it. Apricot Blush, that should go well with the tan carpeting—don't you think?"

"It should work quite well," Lisa agreed.

"Anyway, while I was looking in the

living room closet I found a shoe box way back on the shelf. Had something in it too."

"You found it!" Lisa exclaimed.

"So, it is something you want."

"It certainly is. I've been looking all over for that box. You're a lifesaver Mrs. Hammon. I can hardly wait to get that package back."

"If that's the case you can come get it right now. I'm on my way over to the duplex. I could meet you there."

"I'll be there in ten minutes," Lisa said, anxious to have the statue back in her own hands.

Kay's next question almost sent Lisa into a fit of giggles. "What is it?"

Lisa placed the shoe box on her dresser in her bedroom. Perhaps it was a little sneaky on her part, but she saw no reason to tell Ralph she'd misplaced the statue. It was home now, and she intended to keep a close eye on it.

That evening when she went to bed, Lisa drifted to sleep quickly and slept like a baby.

\* \* \*

Monday passed uneventfully and Tuesday was much the same except for an incident that took place in the library.

Lisa had stopped at the library to browse through the children's book section when she overheard Helen Bogart, the head librarian, in a telephone conversation.

As a regular patron, Lisa was on a first name basis with all the library employees. When Helen hung up the phone, Lisa leaned over to her. "If you wouldn't think me presumptuous, I'd be glad to fill in for your story teller who's having car trouble."

"Oh, Lisa, that would be terrific. The children have already started arriving."

The weather of the Pacific Northwest could be quite unpredictable at times, but the Fourth dawned a beautiful sunny day. Lisa stood looking out the kitchen window, basking in the warmth of the morning sun. It looked as though they were going to have perfect weather for their barbecue and fireworks show. She pushed the curtain back in place, barely able to contain her excitement.

She had just set her empty juice glass in the sink when she heard a knock at the front door. Lisa wasn't surprised to find Grant on her porch, but she was surprised by her reaction. He looked so appealing, dressed in jeans and a light yellow polo shirt. How long had it been since she she'd last seen him?

"Hello," she managed.

Grant smiled. "Good morning, neighbor." A lock of dark hair had fallen across his forehead. His eyes were as bright as the morning sun and for a moment she could only stare at him.

Realizing her behavior was bordering on rudeness, her gaze slid down and rested on Grant's mouth. The sight was just as disturbing, as memories of their first kiss burst forth from her mind. Embarrassed, she quickly looked away, afraid Grant might read her thoughts.

If she had betrayed herself, Grant was gentleman enough not to mention it. "Is there anything I can do to help with the dinner preparations?" he asked.

Lisa took a deep breath and smiled brightly, thankful for a neutral topic. "Everything is taken care of, but thanks for offering."

"Good. That means Todd and I can go pick up the fireworks."

"I think he's ready," Lisa said.

While the fellows were gone Lisa put the

steaks in the marinade and put some eggs on to boil for the potato salad.

Time moved slowly, like a feather floating to the ground, but at last five o'clock came. Grant, with Todd's help arranged the briquettes in the bottom of the grill. Soon the coals were a bright red, and Grant placed the steaks and hot dogs on the grate.

Todd's friend Steve was joining them for dinner, and after they finished doing their fireworks, the boys were going back to Steve's house for the night.

A few feet away, Lisa watched the boys gobbling down hot dogs faster than Grant could cook them. It was a comfortable scene, and childhood memories rushed in upon her. Before her father had died, and when he wasn't working, they used to barbecue almost every weekend of the summer. And she could never get enough hot dogs. She looked over at the boys and smiled. Poor Todd had been too young to store up the good memories of those family barbecues.

While Lisa was lost in dreamland, Grant sidled over and put his arm around her shoulder. "Am I missing something, or is it a private joke?" he whispered in her ear.

She gave him a confused look. "I don't know what you mean."

"Well, you're standing here smiling like you know something the rest of us don't. You're not laughing at my cooking I hope. Otherwise I might be tempted to burn your steak," he teased.

"Oh, it's nothing like that," she apologized. "Just pleasant thoughts from my childhood. We used to barbecue all the time. Then after Dad died—" She lost her voice and couldn't continue.

Grant gave her shoulder a squeeze. "Your dad must have been a great guy."

Lisa blushed. "Sorry, I didn't mean to go all weepy on you."

Leaning down, Grant kissed her forehead. "The cook had better get back to the steaks, before he burns them." With a wink he was gone.

As soon as the first light left the sky, the boys talked Grant into doing the fireworks. Lisa cleared off the picnic table while the guys carried their fireworks around to the front. As soon as she had everything put away she joined them in the front yard.

In the past Lisa had seen a sponsored fireworks show, but she had never been this close to the real thing. She had no idea what to expect, but the safe and sane fireworks more than surpassed her expectation. They were so great she wondered why anyone would bother, or take the chance with illegal fireworks.

Showering sparks of pinks, greens, and reds, along with brilliant flashes of gold illuminated the evening sky. The sight was exhilarating, and Lisa could see why the Fourth of July was so popular with kids.

And the names—they were nearly as intriguing as the fireworks, themselves; and such a variety. The cones especially had interesting tags, such as the Whistling Bird and Happy Flower, the Morning Sunrise, and the Moon and Stars.

Although it wasn't a cone, Lisa's favorite was a small spinner called the Ground Bloom Flower. It whirled inches off the ground while emitting glowing colors of red, green, pink and white, and it lasted a long time too.

And as a fireman's daughter, Lisa was pleased to see that all used fireworks went immediately into a bucket of water.

When the last shot burst forth from a Roman Candle, Grant moved next to Lisa. "I see you're still smiling, so you must be enjoying yourself."

"It was absolutely great," Lisa said, helping Grant carry some of the leftover trash around to the back. "But I feel a little guilty. It must have cost quite a bit. I'm afraid Todd's taken advantage of you."

Grant set the bucket of used fireworks down. "Nonsense. I'll have to confess. I'm the one responsible for most of this stuff."

Lisa's gentle laughter rippled on the air. Once again she had been exposed to the little boy dwelling inside Grant. She could picture him as a youngster, full of enthusiasm, like a young pup yet to experience obedience school, circling back and forth trying to decide what to buy. It was a delightful picture. Of course, he wasn't a child any longer.

Grant turned and looked at her, and their gazes locked. When he held out his arms Lisa went willingly into his embrace, returning his kisses.

He stroked her hair and softly whispered her name. "I never thought I'd feel this way again."

Grant's words jolted her back to reality. Angry with herself, she stepped away, out of his arms. "This won't work," she said, running for the safety of the indoors.

## Chapter Eight

Lisa awoke drained and hollow-eyed. Her late evening encounter with Grant had taken its toll. But, she was now determined, more than ever, to distance herself from Grant.

After last night she realized that even casual, neighborly contact with Grant was impossible. When he was near, her willpower seemed to fly out the window.

Anxious to put all thoughts of her neighbor from her mind, Lisa pushed back the covers and headed for the shower. Story time would keep her busy and her mind off Grant.

As usual Lisa arrived at the church early. Mattie met her in the vestibule. "What's the

matter honey? Did you do too much cele-
brating on the Fourth?"

Lisa laughed. "The Fourth of July would
be a great holiday if it didn't last so long
into the evening." She mentioned nothing
about her restless night due to her neighbor.
Then in an effort to refocus their conversation, Lisa asked Mattie about her day off.

Mattie was telling her about going to the
cemetery when Mrs. Forrester, the mother
of one of their charges, appeared in the doorway. Peggy Forrester was in her early twen-
ties, but a hard life had drained the woman
of any vitality and she looked older. But if
you looked past the droop of her shoulders
you realized she hadn't given up. In spite of
the fact that she and Susan were in a tem-
porary shelter for the homeless Peggy's
voice usually had a ring of optimism.

Lisa admired the woman and tried not to
sound overly solicitous, knowing Peggy
would resent it. Lisa greeted Peggy then
smiled at five-year-old Susan who was
clinging to her mother's hand. Susan was a
shy, reserved child whom Lisa would love
to see laugh more often.

Peggy appeared uneasy and shifted her
stance. "I hate to bother you, but I've got a
bit of a problem. I hope someone here might

be able to help me out." Susan freed her hand from her mother's grip and looked up at Lisa. The child had beautiful brown eyes, Lisa noted, but there was a sadness in their depths.

Lisa suspected Susan had seen too much misery and not enough compassion in her short life time. "I'll be glad to help if I can." Lisa's smile for Susan was especially friendly and the little girl rewarded her with a shy grin.

"I have a job interview this afternoon," Peggy continued, "and I'll be late picking up Susan. Could someone stay with her until I return? I'd be willing to pay." Peggy's voice was calm, but Lisa could see the desperation in the woman's eyes.

Lisa liked Peggy. The woman wanted so much to improve her situation, but at the moment Lisa knew Peggy had no money to spare. If story time hadn't been free, Susan wouldn't be here.

"I'm staying after," Lisa said. "I'll be glad to keep Susan company. That is, if Susan wants to stay with me. She could help me pick out a book for our next story time."

Susan nodded eagerly at Lisa's suggestion.

"Looks like it's settled," Lisa replied.

"Maybe we'll even walk down to the corner for an ice cream cone."

Susan's eyes grew big when Lisa mentioned ice cream. She obviously hadn't had many treats in her life. With a relieved look, Peggy Forrester reached into her purse and pulled out a dollar. "For the ice cream."

Lisa pushed the money away. "Please, you don't need to pay me; the ice cream was my suggestion and my treat."

"Thanks," Peggy said, her eyes shiny with moisture. Leaning down she kissed Susan goodbye. "I'll be back as soon as I can. And please be a good girl for Lisa."

"Good luck with the job interview," Lisa called.

Lisa shoved the last book into her blue tote. "Thanks for your help, Susan. Are you about ready for that ice cream?"

It was a sunny afternoon, perfect for a walk to the ice cream store which was four blocks away. Lisa gazed down at Susan. For once the child's usual reserve had been replaced with delight. Lisa lapsed into a melancholy mood. Would her life have mirrored Susan's if she hadn't been adopted by the Bowmans?

"What kind are you going to have?" Susan asked, breaking into Lisa's musings.

"What?"

"Ice cream. What kind are you going to have?"

"Oh, I don't know yet. How about you?"

"I want a blue one."

"Blue, isn't that bubble gum?"

"Uh-huh. That's what I want."

"Well, if they've got it we'll get you two scoops. How does that sound?" Lisa gave Susan's hand a squeeze.

"Good."

Todd was watching TV when Lisa arrived home. "Sorry I'm late, but I stayed after to help a friend."

Todd turned off the TV. "That's okay, but I think you'd better sit down. You got a package a while ago."

Visions of the last package she'd received came to mind. With a groan she sank down onto the sofa. *Had Ralph sent another of his great finds?*

When Todd handed her the long florist box a surge of guilt washed over her. Flowers! He had sent flowers.

Ralph would often send her flowers when she helped with his overload of typing, but this, this was unexpected. Lisa tugged at the red ribbon, and in her excitement managed to knot the satiny cord. Finally, after several attempts, the ribbon fell free of the box. Her heart beat wildly against her chest as she lifted the lid.

Roses! Her favorite. Ralph had never before gotten her roses. She sighed softly, removing the dozen long-stemmed beauties from the bed of tissue paper. How positively romantic. This was much better than an ugly statue.

Lisa leaned down, inhaling the flowers' sweet fragrance. When she did, a flash of white in the corner of the box caught her eyes. Carefully returning the roses to the box she removed the card.

*Thanks for making my Fourth-SPEC-TACULAR!*

*Grant*

Surprised, Lisa stared at the card. The flowers weren't from Ralph.

"Hey, Sis." Todd said, dropping down on the other end of the sofa. "I think Grant kind of likes you. Wouldn't it be neat if the two of you got married? Then we could be a real family." His whole face spread into a smile.

Lisa jerked to attention. Married? She let out a quiet sigh. "I'm afraid that's out of the question, Todd."

Todd looked crestfallen. "Why not? He likes you. I know he does." The cheerfulness had left his voice.

*How could she make Todd understand?* "Todd, I know you like Grant a lot, but he and I have nothing in common. Besides, I'm going to marry someone else."

Todd's eyes darkened. "You can't do that."

Lisa bit her lower lip. *She knew he wouldn't understand.* "Honey, I know Grant is your friend, but he isn't right for me, and like I said I'm going to marry someone else."

Looking betrayed, Todd rose from the sofa with a stiff angry jerk. "I suppose you're going to married that guy that sent you the statue?"

"Yes, I am. Ralph's very nice, and once you meet him I'm sure you'll like him too. You needn't worry...no one is going to ask you give up your friendship with Grant."

"Sure," Todd said, stomping from the room. The door to his bedroom banged shut.

Lisa looked at the crimson roses—they were beautiful. Although she had resolved to stay away from Grant, she would have to thank him for the flowers. After putting the roses in a vase she sat down at her desk and pulled out a sheet of paper. A letter was the cowardly way out, but she simply couldn't face him—not yet.

Before sealing the envelope Lisa read the note one last time.

*Grant,*
*The roses are beautiful, but you really shouldn't have. You've already done enough for Todd and me. I don't want you to feel obligated to us.*

*Lisa B.*

Satisfied the note was polite and impersonal Lisa tucked it inside the envelope and walked next door. She knew Grant wasn't home so she wedged it between the screen door and the frame.

Feeling like a fraud and a coward she tried justifying her actions. After all, Grant was going to be busy the next few days working on a case. If she waited to thank him in person it might take a while. Her pep talk, however, could not erase the fact that she did not have the courage to look him in the face.

As it turned out, exactly five days passed

before Lisa saw Grant again. It was evening and she was in the back yard removing towels from the clothesline.

She hadn't heard him approaching, and when he said her name it was too late to run. Reluctantly she turned, knowing that tonight would probably be the turning point in their friendship.

For once even Grant seemed at a loss for words. "I got your note."

Lisa released the wooden clothespins in her hand and they tumbled into the basket with barely a sound. "The flowers were beautiful. Thank you."

Time stood still as the quiet summer evening settled in around Lisa and Grant, enfolding them into their own private world. They stood awkwardly, each waiting for the other to speak.

Grant was the first to break silence. "I hope you know I don't see you and Todd as an obligation. On the contrary, I feel very fortunate to have the two of you as neighbors." The corner of his mouth lifted in a grin.

Lisa looked away. She had to, before she found herself weakening. That charming little half-grin of his had a way of undermining her resistance. "W . . . we can't be taking advantage of you all the time. You've got a life of your own to live."

Grant reached out, placing one hand on her shoulder, the other hand he cupped beneath her chin forcing Lisa to look at him.

"Have I done something to offend you?" he asked. "You seem to be shying away from me; like the other night."

"It's not your fault." She tried looking away, but Grant wouldn't let her. "I—It's—" She was mumbling now. "We can never be anything but friends." *There, at last it was out.*

Grant's left eyebrow shot up and his gaze bore into her, refusing to let go. He dropped his hands, as if he knew she was incapable of escaping. "Why is that?"

She side-stepped the truth, or at least the whole truth. "I . . . there's someone else."

"I see," he said, studying her. "Do you love him?"

Lisa wrung her hands. Love? What was love? Ralph was good to her and they got along. Wasn't that love? "I'm going to be married."

Grant persisted. "You didn't answer my question, but that's okay. I think I've got my answer." There was a rebuking tone to his words.

Lisa's temper flared ever so slightly. How dare he judge her. It was her life and her decision. "I'm not sure what you're getting at, but I'm going to be married this fall."

"After the way you kissed me the other night, you may be getting married, but you're certainly not in love with the guy." With that Grant turned and walked away.

Furious, Lisa yelled at his back. "And to think I was hoping we could still be friends."

He pivoted, a hurt expression on his face. "Of course we can be friends. And as your friend I'm offering a bit of advice. Don't marry the guy if you don't love him. A man deserves better than that."

Lisa opened her mouth to speak, but Grant had disappeared inside. "I'm not sure I want to be your friend," she whispered. She liked and respected Ralph, wasn't that what a marriage needed? But like a bad toothache, Grant's words stayed with her all night, ruining her sleep.

She saw nothing of Grant for the next few days, although she knew Todd had seen him. It was just as well, she told herself, for she was having a difficult time dealing with Todd's feelings and didn't need any confrontations with Grant. Her brother was not ready to forgive her for rejecting Grant, and the strain was wearing on her nerves. She could only hope that once Todd met Ralph things would improve.

Still in her pajamas and robe, Lisa was reading the morning newspaper and drinking a cup of coffee when the telephone rang. At first she didn't recognize Beth's voice then recognition dawned. "Beth. How nice to hear from you."

"I'm sorry to disturb you," Beth said, her voice sounding shaky.

"Is everything all right?" Lisa asked. It was much too early in the morning for just a friendly conversation.

"I just got a call from Grant's superiors." There was a pause. "It'll be on the noon news. Grant's been injured."

For a moment Lisa was too stunned to speak. She felt as though someone had slugged her in the stomach, knocking all the air from her lungs. "What?" Maybe she had misunderstood.

As Beth repeated herself, Lisa felt her legs giving away. She quickly moved to the sofa and sat down. "What happened?"

"Grant and another officer were on a stakeout of a robbery suspect. When they tried to arrest the guy Grant was shot. That's all I know at this time." Her voice sounded fragile and scared. "I just thought you and Todd would like to know before you hear about it on TV."

"Shot?" Lisa nearly dropped the phone. "How bad is it?"

"They've got to remove a bullet from his leg, but other than that I don't think it's serious. The other officer escaped injury, and the suspect's in jail."

"Oh, Beth, I'm so sorry." This was exactly why she didn't want to become romantically involved with Grant. The daily worry would be too much. "Is there anything I can do?"

"Not at the moment, but thanks for asking. I just didn't want you to hear about it on the news." Lisa could tell Beth was trying not to cry.

"Well then, is there anything I can do for you?" Lisa asked.

"I'm fine. I'll be driving down in just a bit, and I'm going to stay at Grant's, so we can talk some more when I arrive."

"Please be careful," Lisa said before hanging up the phone. Her next problem was how to tell Todd.

Todd took the news better than Lisa expected. He was anxious to see Grant, but accepted the fact he probably couldn't see Grant until tomorrow.

When Beth's little yellow car pulled into the driveway, Lisa and Todd rushed outside to meet her. After a tearful embrace, the three of them went inside.

Lisa set a cup of coffee in front Beth. She couldn't help noticing the pretty young model was taking her brother's injury harder than she was letting on. Even her blue designer suit seemed to hang listlessly on her slender figure. "If there's anything, anything at all that I can do to help out, just let me know."

"When do you think I can see him?" Todd asked.

Beth took a sip of coffee. "If he's allowed visitors, I'll take you tomorrow."

Lisa poured some more coffee in her cup then set the pot back on the stove. "Tell us what you know."

"The doctor I talked to said Grant's injuries weren't life-threatening. But he was very lucky. A bullet just grazed his head and the wound to his leg looks pretty clean, but, of course, they have to remove the bullet." Absentmindedly, Beth stirred her coffee. "If there's no infection he shouldn't be down too long."

As Lisa fought back tears of relief, thoughts she hadn't intended to say spilled from her mouth. "Does Grant have any idea how hard this is on you? Is his job so important to him?" She regretted her slip of the tongue immediately, but it was too late to take it back. "I'm sorry. I had no right."

Beth reached across the table and patted Lisa's hand in sympathy. "The first time is the hardest."

Lisa inhaled sharply as if seized by pain. "First time?"

"Yes, I'm afraid this isn't the first close call he's had," Beth said. "But to Grant it's just part of his job. After awhile you learn to accept it because he does."

Beth's frankness was like a bolt of lightning to Lisa's heart. She knew she'd never be able to accept his job. She raised her cup to take a drink, but her hand was so unsteady she set it back down, only to have it tip, sending coffee across the table. The sleeve of Beth's blue suit turned a spotted brown.

"Oh, I'm sorry," Lisa said, grabbing a towel and dabbing at the stains.

Beth took the towel from Lisa's hands. "Forget it. We're all a little upset. Besides, I was going to change clothes anyway before going to the hospital. The doctor said I could see Grant when he came out of surgery. He probably won't be awake, but I'm the only family he's got. I feel I should be there." Beth stood and gave Lisa a hug. "I'll talk to you when I return."

Lisa walked her to the door. "Tell Grant we said hello."

"I will, but I'm sure he'll be allowed visitors tomorrow."

Feeling totally drained, Lisa walked back to the kitchen and placed their dirty cups in the sink. If she had any doubts before, this incident substantiated her fears. She could not handle Grant's job. Just being his friend would be tough enough.

It was as a friend that Lisa pulled her Chevy into the hospital parking lot, the next afternoon. Under her left arm was a Sports Illustrated, and in her right hand was a small wrapped package containing a hand-held battery-operated game. It should help to pass the time. Beth had told her last night that Grant was being detained for several more days. The doctors were afraid his injured leg might become infected, and they wanted to keep an eye on it.

Lisa stepped from the elevator out onto the fourth floor. Outside room 402 she paused long enough to take a deep breath.

She hadn't seen Grant since their argument and she was nervous. After another deep breath she found the courage to enter his room.

Grant was facing the window when she walked in, and Lisa thought he might be sleeping, but as if sensing the presence of someone he turned towards the doorway. His face looked a little pale beneath a day's growth of beard.

Lisa stared. It was a shock seeing him look so weak. He looked young and vulnerable wearing a white hospital gown and with a bandage on his forehead. She wanted to reach out and hug him, make sure he was all right, but somehow she resisted. She moved toward his bed. "How are you feeling?"

"I'm going to live."

"That's good. Otherwise, I'd have to return this," she teased, handing him the brown and yellow striped package.

"What's this?"

"Just a little something to help you get through the next few days." Turning the straight-back wooden chair so it was facing the bed, Lisa sat down. "I brought you something to read when you're tired of the game," she said, placing the magazine on the night table.

"Thanks," Grant said, tearing the brown and yellow paper. His face brightened when he saw the game. "I'm sure this should make my stay a little more enjoyable." He balled up the paper and tossed it toward a waste can in the corner of the room, making the basket.

"Not bad for someone's who's bedridden, huh?" Then he gave her that charming smile of his.

Why, Lisa wondered, could one small grin from this guy set her pulse racing. "Great. Just great."

Lisa cleared her throat and smiled. *What to say? She couldn't remember feeling this tongue-tied since she was a teenager.*

Grant spoke, breaking the awkward silence that had settled over the room. "I didn't think you'd come."

"Don't be silly. Why wouldn't I come?"

He ignored her question. "Are you still getting married?"

Her back stiffened at the accusing tone of his voice. "Of course."

"When I held you in my arms the other night your kisses were for me—not some other guy. Will you deny that?"

"The other night was a mistake. I shouldn't have encouraged you. We have no future together."

"Why?" he asked softly. "Be truthful this time."

"You want the truth! Okay. The truth is I can't handle your job. Look at you! You were lucky this time. Next time you might not survive. I won't live with that kind of fear day in and day out."

If she thought Grant looked pale when she walked into his room, he looked absolutely ghostly now.

"I see. Life is not without its worries and little insecurities, Lisa. I only wish you'd told me sooner. And you're right—we have no future together." There was a ring of finality to his words.

Lisa rose quickly, hoping to leave before Grant noticed the tears that were about to spill from her eyes.

"I hope you find what you're looking for," he said as she stepped into the hall.

## Chapter Nine

When she reached her car Lisa wiped her eyes. This time she knew for certain that what ever might have been between her and Grant was over. It was best this way, but still it hurt.

She never returned to visit Grant after that, but she knew from listening to Todd and Beth that Grant was recovering and would soon be released from the hospital.

If Beth was curious about the dissension between her brother and Lisa, Beth didn't ask. A mellowed Todd was also taking the estrangement without comment. Lisa couldn't help wondering if Grant had talked to the two of them, but whatever the reason she was glad for their silence.

The day Grant came home from the hospital, Beth stopped to say goodbye. But other than asking Lisa to keep an eye on Grant and to call if he was having any problems, his name was not mentioned. Lisa quickly agreed to help out, figuring that with Todd's help she wouldn't have to have any personal contact with Grant.

Later that afternoon when Todd returned from next door, Lisa was surprised to learn Grant was leaving for a two-week stay at the beach to recuperate from his injury.

Her concern must have showed on her face. "Grant said not to worry, his doctor told him to get a little sun." Todd handed her a paper with a list of phone numbers for a plumber, electrician, and general handyman.

"Grant said if we had any problems while he's gone we're to call one of these guys."

Lisa took the paper and taped it to the cupboard door. *So, Grant was going away.* That was fine with her, maybe now she could get her life back on track. And, maybe when he returned from the beach their relationship would be back to where it belonged—friend and neighbor.

Although, she truly wondered if they would ever be able to revert back to such friendly rapport. Over the last few days she had given the matter considerable thought and had concluded it might be easier to move again. That was her last option, of course, and only time would tell how things would work out. Besides, once she married Ralph, she and Todd would be gone.

But, for the moment she was glad Grant was leaving town. Now she could concentrate on Ralph's return, which was only a few days away. He had called again last night to remind her of his arrival Saturday evening. He had jokingly asked if she was involved in any crises that would prevent her from meeting his plane which was due in about six.

She had laughed half-heartedly at his attempted humor, wondering if he would ever forget she hadn't stood him up by choice.

Lisa's emotions were mixed on Friday as she prepared for work. Just one more day and Ralph would be home. She was excited and just a wee bit nervous about their reunion. She was eager to see Ralph, but his arrival would signify a change in her life. The thought of marrying left her feeling just a little edgy, but then, didn't all brides-to-be feel this way?

She was certain her uneasiness would disappear as soon as the wedding was behind them. Humming to herself, she searched her purse for her car keys.

Lisa knocked, then leaned into Todd's room. She was pleased and surprised to see him reading the Jack London novel she had suggested he read. "Now remember, don't make any plans for tomorrow evening. We'll be leaving for the airport about five."

Todd lowered his book. "Gee, Sis, I don't see why I have to go with you."

He had been complaining from the moment she asked him to accompany her to the airport. Even though he hadn't actually said anything, Lisa suspected he was still hoping she and Grant would get together. This naturally made her brother a little prejudiced towards Ralph.

Lisa sighed. "Todd, we've been through this before. Ralph and I are going to be married, and the sooner the two of you meet the better. I know it'll take awhile to become good friends, but it's important to me that the two of you get along."

"Okay. I'll go. All right?" Todd's tone left little doubt as to his true feelings. As an afterthought he added, "What if Grant calls? He said he'd call me."

Lisa's eyebrows arched slightly. "If he misses you I'm sure he'll try again. I doubt he expects you to put your life on hold waiting for his call."

Her words were greeted with silence, but Lisa didn't miss the faint scowl that appeared on Todd's face.

The morning moved quickly for Lisa and before long she was closing the cover on a book about a dog named Clifford. As she lined the children up to go downstairs for lunch Mattie motioned to her from the back of the room.

Laying aside the book she was holding, Lisa stepped over to her friend. "What's up? Do you need more time to get ready before I bring the children down for lunch?" She could easily read another short story.

"I'm afraid I've got some bad news. I just got a call from the hospital. It seems Peggy Forrester has been injured in an accident and won't be able to pick up Susan. I think we'll have to notify the police so they can place the child in a foster home until her mom is able to care for her again."

Lisa gasped. Mattie's words were a complete surprise. "How terrible. I hope her injuries aren't serious." Having just started a new job, the poor woman was just beginning to get on her feet financially. Lisa knew Peggy hoped to move into her own place soon, and now this had to happen. And what about Susan?

Lisa glanced at Susan. How would she survive this setback? "Let's take the children downstairs, Mattie. Then you can tell me all about it."

After the children were settled for lunch, Mattie filled in the rest of the details for Lisa. "Peggy was hit by a car while crossing the street. I don't know the extent of her injuries, but she was conscious and asked the hospital to call us. I feel sorry for Susan, but I guess we have no choice but to notify the police."

"That won't be necessary," Lisa declared. "There's no way I'm going to let that child be sent off to live with strangers." Lisa had always had a soft spot for children, and she wasn't about to stand by while Susan was placed in foster care. Being separated from her mother would be hard enough on the child. The child needed familiar faces and friends right now.

"After lunch I'll call the hospital to talk to Peggy. If it's all right with her, Susan can stay with me until her mom's released.

But I want Susan to talk to her mom, so she knows she needs permission before going away with someone, even a friend."

Mattie stepped over to Lisa and hugged her. "Girl, you've got a heart of an angel. I know her mother will rest much easier knowing Susan's with you."

"It's all set," Lisa told Mattie as she hung up the phone. Lisa placed an arm around Susan, who looked dazed, drawing her near. "I'm going to take Susan by the shelter so we can pick up her belongings, then we're going to stop by the hospital. They said Susan could see her mom for a few minutes."

At the shelter Lisa explained the circumstances to those in charge and left her name, address and telephone number in case there was a need to contact her.

Holding Susan's hand, and carrying a brown grocery bag, which contained Susan's few belongings, Lisa stepped out into the afternoon sun. She felt like crying. Children deserved more than a bed, a meal, and a brown bag for their possessions.

At the hospital, a nurse with a friendly face escorted Lisa and Susan to Mrs. Forrester's room. Peggy was awake when they entered, but she did look groggy with medication. Her left arm was in a cast, and her left leg was in traction. Small cuts and bruises covered much of the rest of her body.

"You look tired," Lisa said.

Peggy smiled. "Some, but I couldn't go to sleep before seeing my little girl," she said, from beneath half-closed eyes. "Come here and give mommy a kiss, Susan."

Susan rushed to her mother's bedside, and Lisa held her up so she could kiss Peggy's cheek. Lisa hoped Mrs. Forrester's appearance wouldn't be too traumatic for Susan, but the brief visit seemed to uplift both mother and child, and Peggy's assurance that she was going to be okay brought a smile to Susan's face.

"I can't thank you enough, Lisa," Peggy said. "It's such a big relief knowing Susan is staying with you. If there's anything I can do for you when I get out of here, please let me know."

"I will," Lisa said trying to put Peggy at ease. "But right now I only want you to think about getting better."

"Time's up," called the nurse from the doorway.

Lisa handed Peggy a paper with her phone number. "Call anytime you feel like it."

Peggy squeezed Lisa's hand. "Thanks for caring." Then Peggy kissed Susan goodbye.

At the nurse's station, Lisa left her name and phone number with instructions to call if Peggy needed anything or if her condition should worsen.

Susan was quiet on the drive home. Lisa reached over and patted the child's leg. She looked so small and forlorn buckled into the passenger's seat. To her chest she clutched a limp rag doll with red yarn hair. Whether Susan clung to the doll out of love, or because it was the only toy she had, Lisa couldn't be sure. Either way, it was a heart-wrenching scene.

"I know this must be a scary time for you," Lisa said, "but your mommie is going to be all right. It's just going to take awhile." She had hoped to offer some reassurance, but there was little change in expression on Susan's face. "I think we can have a lot of fun together," she continued.

"I know," Susan said.

"You aren't going to be staying with me forever, just until your momma is able to leave the hospital. In the mean time we'll keep in touch with her."

The corner of Susan's mouth twitched and Lisa thought she was making progress.

"Maybe we could go to the florist tomorrow and pick out some flowers for her. What do you think of that idea?"

Susan nodded, her expression brightened considerably.

"Good. We'll take her a pretty bouquet tomorrow."

Lisa slowed and signaled for a right turn, pulling into a fast food restaurant. "How about hamburgers for dinner?" Lisa was pleased to see that this suggestion brought a wide smile to Susan's face.

Todd was shooting baskets in the driveway when they arrived home with dinner. He and Susan took an immediate liking to one another in spite of their age difference. Smiling to herself, Lisa hoped they would continue to get along without any bickering.

Saturday turned out to be a very busy day. Early in the morning, Lisa and Susan went to the florist and picked out a huge bouquet of flowers which they personally delivered to Peggy at the hospital. After that they stopped at a department store where Lisa purchased a toothbrush, a comb and brush, and a pair of pajamas for Susan.

Although Lisa considered these necessary items, Susan acted as though this was her one and only shopping trip and each purchase her last. Lisa stood patiently by for ten minutes as Susan debated between a yellow or pink toothbrush. The comb and brush took another ten minutes and the pajamas took three times as long, but Lisa didn't have the heart to rush her.

By the time they got home Lisa's feet were killing her and if she hadn't promised to meet Ralph's plane she would have had an early dinner and gone to bed.

Lisa sat in the airport waiting area, stifling a yawn. She was afraid she'd fall asleep if Ralph's plane didn't arrive soon. Todd and Susan had gone off in search of a pop machine and the nearly empty lounge was too quiet. In an attempt to stay awake Lisa picked up the newspaper from the vacant chair next to her. Maybe if she read she could stay awake. But after several attempts to focus her eyes she put the paper back.

Looking up, she smiled when she saw Ralph coming toward her. There was a slight frown on his face. She was sure he hadn't spotted her by the way he kept glancing around the terminal.

He looked very tan after his summer in

the sun. The tan accentuated the blue of his eyes and his black hair gleamed in the overhead lights. He made quite a striking figure dressed in gray slacks and navy blue sport coat. Lisa stood up and waved.

When he saw her he smiled, the frown leaving his face. She knew he was pleased to see her, but to Lisa's surprise Ralph's smile had little effect upon her. For some reason, another face and another smile came into her mind. Grant. For one second she wondered what he was doing.

*Stop that!* she chastised herself. She didn't want to think about Grant. The man who had asked her to marry him was coming toward her. She didn't want to spoil his homecoming with thoughts of her neighbor.

Lisa stretched out her arms and welcomed Ralph into her embrace, turning her cheek for his kiss.

"What a way to welcome me home. Don't I deserve a real kiss?" Ralph complained. "After all, we are engaged."

"Sorry, Ralph. I guess I'm just tired. I had a very busy day."

His eyes darkened. "I hope you're not too tired to stop by my parents' on the way home. I thought we'd break the news to them about our marriage plans."

She hadn't meant to groan, but it was over and done with before she could stop it. "Not tonight, Ralph. I'm too tired and . . . something came up."

Ralph said something under his breath which Lisa didn't understand, but she knew he wasn't happy by the curl of his upper lip. "What have you gotten yourself mixed up in now?"

From the corner of her eye Lisa could see Todd and Susan off in the distance. She nodded in their direction. "I've got the kids with me."

"Kids?"

"My brother and Susan. Susan's mother is in the hospital so Susan will be staying with me for awhile. Why don't you stop by my place? I'm going to make some popcorn and we can put a tape in the VCR and watch a movie."

"A foursome. How cozy. I think I'll pass. Maybe you can work me into your schedule later on. Or will something come up?"

Hurt, Lisa stepped back from Ralph. "You make it sound like I deliberately spoiled your plans."

"Maybe not deliberately, but I've been gone for six weeks. Do you honestly expect me to be thrilled about an evening of popcorn, TV, and kids? I was looking forward to some time alone with you."

"Well, if we went to your parents' house, we certainly wouldn't be alone. I can't see the difference. What's the matter, don't you like children?"

There was a challenge in Ralph's eyes. "It seems to me, you've got your priorities mixed up a bit."

Lisa counted to ten. She was losing her temper. "Oh, for crying out loud, Ralph, don't go making a mountain out of a mole hill. Now, here come the kids. I don't want to discuss this anymore."

Ralph looked suspiciously at the kids as they approached. "They don't bite," Lisa quipped, tugging at his hand. "Come on, let me introduce you."

Ralph acknowledged the kids with a thin smile and a nod, which the kids returned in kind. Taking Lisa's elbow, Ralph stepped away from the kids. His gaze was icy cold. "I think you'd better just take me home tonight."

Lisa quickly agreed.

"How about tomorrow?" Ralph asked, his tone callous. "Are you going to be free tomorrow evening—or are you going to be too busy to make time for me?"

By now her anger had cooled and a good dose of guilt was beginning to take its place. "I'll be free."

"Good. I'll call my mother. Plan on dinner at their house." With an impatient movement he reached for his suitcases.

Lisa stepped around Ralph. "Come along kids."

On the drive back to Tacoma Ralph apologized, or at least Lisa took it as an apology. "You're probably right. Tomorrow might be better for both of us." Ralph slanted a glance at Lisa. "A good night's rest in my own bed might be just what I need."

Lisa smiled in agreement, remembering how tired and cranky she was after two weeks on the sofa. Stopping in front of Ralph's apartment, Lisa got out of the car so Ralph could remove his luggage from the truck.

She was sure Ralph was going to kiss her goodnight when a giggle came from inside the car. Instead, he merely brushed his lips against her cheek.

After dropping Ralph off at his place Lisa and the kids went home and popped some corn and watched TV. It was a pleasant evening and Lisa enjoyed herself. Although she wasn't overly excited about dinner with the senior Mr. and Mrs. Trenton, she would devote the entire evening tomorrow to Ralph.

And if Ralph wanted to spend the whole evening with his parents—she hoped he wouldn't—somehow she'd manage. Ralph's parents weren't the easiest people to associate with. As far as Lisa was concerned they were one step away from being snobby, but then if she had their money maybe she'd be a little uppish too. What bothered Lisa the most, however, was the way their opinions and attitude rubbed off on Ralph after a couple of hours of socializing. Lisa grimaced. She'd have to work on her own attitude if she was going to become their daughter-in-law.

Ralph picked Lisa up at seven o'clock and drove toward the Lakewood district, where his parents owned a big two-story house. From earlier visits, Lisa knew the house had at least ten or twelve rooms. The back yard even had an enclosed swimming pool. Ralph's father was a retired banker, and over the years he had obviously invested his money well.

Lisa smiled sweetly at Ralph. Whatever it took she was determined their evening would go smoothly. After yesterday, she felt she owed him a little something extra. His words about making time for him had left her feeling more than a bit guilty.

Her determination to please Ralph dimmed, however, when he spoke. "I don't know how you do it Lisa, but you sure manage to get yourself involved in one problem after another. How did you get talked into babysitting for the next few weeks? Doesn't this woman have any family who can babysit?"

Lisa ignored his haughty tone. "First of all I didn't get talked into anything. I volunteered. And no the woman doesn't have anyone to help her."

"Volunteered?" Ralph shook his head, as if he couldn't believe what he was hearing. "Lisa my girl, the average person does not volunteer to take on someone's kid for an undetermined amount of time. You can go ahead and try to save the world if you want, but after we're married don't try to involve me in any of your escapades."

Lisa glanced at Ralph. There was a rigid set to his jaw. "Thanks for your permission," she snapped. "You needn't worry about becoming involved in my ventures. I wouldn't impose." They hadn't even arrived at the

Trentons' and already Lisa could sense a change in Ralph's attitude.

A loud hmph brought Lisa back to the present. "Did you say something?" she asked.

Ralph cleared his throat again. "As a matter of fact I did. I was wondering if you can find the time to look for a ring tomorrow."

"I think that can be arranged," Lisa said as he pulled the Pontiac Firebird up the long circular drive.

The closer they got to the large two-story house the more apprehensive Lisa became.

When Joyce Trenton opened the door and stepped out to the porch, a sharp pain crawled up the back of Lisa's neck. Lisa returned the woman's anemic wave, and opened her purse to check for some aspirin.

## Chapter Ten

Ralph held the door open and Lisa stepped outside, forcing herself to smile. As usual, Mrs. Trenton's greeting was cordial and polite, but again Lisa felt as though she were a commoner in the presence of nobility.

Lisa sighed. She really didn't want to sound so ungracious. Other than her patronizing manner Joyce was a nice person.

Joyce Trenton kissed Ralph on the cheek. "Good evening son. I thought you might come see us last night." She didn't wait for an answer, but turned to Lisa.

"Come in my dear," Joyce crooned. "We've just enough time for a cocktail before dinner."

"Thanks." Lisa obligingly accompanied her hostess inside the gleaming marble tiled foyer while Ralph and his father followed.

They entered, through double doors, into a sitting room of brocade, polished wood and sparkling silver. A bouquet of fresh flowers adorned the coffee table that was positioned in front of a wheat-colored sofa. The room looked as though it came straight off the pages of a decorator's magazine, but even the bright splashes of yellow and purple flowers could not soften the overall effect. It wasn't a room Lisa could be comfortable in for very long at a time. She thought of her own living room where the coffee table was covered with magazines and an assortment of Todd's trading cards, and in the corner of the sofa, Susan's doll waited patiently.

Until this evening Lisa had ignored—intentionally or unintentionally—the differences between what was Ralph's accustomed life-style and her own. She glanced around the room again; nothing was out of place. Even the bowl of flowers looked as though it had been precisely centered on the mahogany table. She imagine they would be replaced at the first signs of a drooping petal. If this was the way Ralph expected to live after they were married she had some major adjusting to do.

A flash of light drew Lisa's attention away from the silver bowl of flowers to a curio cabinet across the room. A shaft of evening sunlight filtering in through the sheer window curtains reflected on a collection of small crystal figurines inside the cabinet. Lisa walked over to examine the delicate trinkets which were Joyce Trenton's hobby. Knowing Joyce had a weakness for the beautiful glass knick-knacks at least made her seem more approachable.

Although Lisa had seen the collection before, she still stopped to admire the tiny crystal creations. "Oh, I see you've added a new piece," she said, spotting a tiny baby bird in a woven nest of clear glass. "It's lovely."

Joyce smiled at Lisa's praise. "Yes, it is nice isn't it? Ralph sent it to me while he was away. He's always so thoughtful that way."

Grinning, Ralph moved next to Lisa and handed her a glass of white wine. "You should see the statue I got Lisa, Mother. It wasn't an original, but it was a magnificent copy of one of the island gods. Isn't it nice, sweetheart?"

Lisa looked up at Ralph, and with a smile on her face she lied. "Yes, it is."

Joyce beamed. "It's so nice that the two of you share the same interests. Ralph's always trying to get me interested in his artifacts, but I keep telling him I'm too old and set in my ways to change the decor of the house."

Mrs. Trenton was usually a doting mother to her only child so her comment was a surprise. Lisa could only guess that at one time Ralph had presented his mother with a gift similar to 'old triangle head,' and she had become too 'old' to change her decor.

"Lisa's learning to appreciate my work," Ralph said, leaning over and kissing her on the forehead. "Of course, after we're married Lisa will share in all my fine collectibles and I'm sure her knowledge will grow. I may even take her on a dig with me."

The word married grabbed Joyce's attention and her eyes widened with astonishment. "Married?" There was an edge to her voice.

*She doesn't think I'm good enough.* Lisa tried to keep her thoughts from registering on her face.

"When is this wedding going to take place?" Joyce asked.

Ralph placed his arm around Lisa's shoulder and drew her near. "Soon."

"Oh, my, I hope you're not going to rush into anything." Joyce's voice sounded near panic.

Phillip Trenton, who looked very much like a retired bank president with his white hair and mustache, spoke up. "Now, dear, the kids have known each other for over a year. In fact, I'd say it's time Ralph settled down."

Joyce's complexion turned a slight pink under her makeup and her lips stretched out into a thin line. She had obviously expected more support from her husband.

"I—well, I . . . we just need some time to do a proper wedding. You know we don't want to rush into this. There's a certain procedure one needs to follow when doing a wedding. I do not wish to be embarrassed in front of my friends."

Perturbed, Phillip cleared his throat. "I think most of our friends would understand even if the kids elope. It's only that group you play bridge with that will keep a score card."

Even though she could see no reason to hurry the wedding, Lisa was appreciative of Phillip's support.

Joyce shook her head disapprovingly. "Men! You don't understand. There's a matter of arranging for a caterer, a church, and of course, a dress. Things must be done correctly if you're going to make the right impression." She turned to Lisa. "Isn't that true?"

Feeling trapped, Lisa merely gave a brief nod.

As if Lisa had given the right answer, Mrs. Trenton walked over and gave her a big hug. In spite of Joyce's earlier indifference, Lisa realized Joyce had nothing against her. She was just concerned about making the proper impression so she wouldn't be embarrassed. However, once Joyce had accepted their upcoming marriage her enthusiasm poured forth.

"Have you thought about the colors you're going to use? Yellows and golds are nice for a fall wedding."

Lisa shook her head.

"We can have the reception at the country club. I'll be glad to handle the arrangements," Joyce said.

"That will be super, Mother. Since Lisa has no one to help her, I'm sure any assistance you can give her will be appreciated."

Ralph turned to Lisa, "Isn't that right, sweetheart?"

Again Lisa found herself speechless and barely able to smile. *What had gone wrong? Things were getting completely out of hand.*

Without waiting for Lisa's response, Joyce seemed to take Ralph's offer as an accepted fact. "You can count on my help, Lisa. Why, I know the perfect place to shop for your gown. Anne Marie's has one-of-a-kind dresses."

Lisa didn't want to get off on the wrong foot with her future mother-in-law, but she was sorely afraid her budget could not afford a dress from Anne Marie's. "Thanks," she murmured, sidestepping a confrontation. Later she would mention her limited budget.

"Well, now that we've got that settled, I think it's time we ate. I'll tell Mavis we're ready for dinner." Mrs. Trenton's steely blue gaze met Lisa's. "But after dinner we'll discuss the wedding plans some more."

Somehow, Lisa made it through dinner, but by the time dessert was served her head felt as though a rock band had taken up residence.

"Have you decided upon a ring?" she heard Joyce ask.

"I thought we'd go shopping for one tomorrow," Ralph answered his mother.

"Before you decide, you might want to look at the set of rings in our safety deposit box." Joyce looked at Lisa. "Phillip got me a new set of rings two years ago for our anniversary, but I haven't had the heart to get rid of my original rings." Joyce smiled sweetly at her husband. "But if you were to wear them they'd still be in the family."

Lisa was barely able to swallow her last bite of cherry cobbler. *She certainly didn't want to wear Joyce Trenton's rings.*

"What a terrific idea," Ralph exclaimed before Lisa could decline Joyce's offer.

Feeling as though she'd been caught in a whirlpool, Lisa pushed away from the table. "Please, you'll have to excuse me, but I've got a terrible headache."

A little frown crossed Mrs. Trenton's forehead. "Would you like some aspirin my dear? I can have Mavis bring you some."

Fighting back rising frustrations, Lisa answered politely. "Thanks, but I really feel as though I need to go home."

Quietly projecting himself, Phillip spoke. "I think your prospective bride has had too much excitement, Ralph. Perhaps you should take her home. There will be ample opportunity in the future for us to dine together."

Lisa looked across the table to Phillip and smiled her thanks. *Now if Ralph would just heed his father's advice.*

But Mrs. Trenton wasn't about to let Lisa go without making a final comment. "I hope this doesn't happen often," she said, eyeing Lisa uncertainly. "Now isn't the time to come down with something. It would be terribly inconvenient. You're going to need all your energy to plan this wedding properly."

*Yes,* Lisa thought, *the wedding.* She would like to have said, *then you can handle it for me,* but she held her tongue.

Joyce's falsetto voice cut into Lisa's musings. "Perhaps you should see a doctor? I could make you an appointment with our physician. I'm sure Dr. Baldwin would see you if I asked him as a favor to me."

Lisa lightly rubbed her forehead with her fingers. "I don't think that will be necessary. It's just a headache. I'm sure it'll be gone by tomorrow."

Ralph gave Lisa a look of dismay, then told Phillip and Joyce, "She's been so busy worrying about everyone else, she forgets to take time out for herself."

Lisa cringed. She hoped Ralph wouldn't

feel compelled to tell his parents about Susan. Ralph thought that Lisa was being taken advantage of. "You hardly know this Peggy Forrester," he reminded Lisa. Time and again she had explained that she had volunteered to watch Susan, but her explanation fell on deaf ears.

"Is that right," Joyce commented.

That was all the encouragement Ralph needed. "In addition to having Todd to take care of, Lisa let herself be manipulated into taking on five-year-old Susan."

"My, my, dear, you must remember you can't solve the problems of the world all by yourself," Joyce offered dryly.

Even Phillip, the quieter of the Trentons had some advice for her. "If you let people get away with using you once, they'll come back again and again." Phillip's mustache twitched. "You mustn't let sentimentality get in the way of clear thinking. That was one of the first things I had to learn when I started out in banking."

Lisa wanted to shout that she had not been manipulated, nor would she become a doormat for anyone, but she believed in helping someone out, who, through no fault of their own was experiencing hard times. But as she glanced around at the three

Trentons sitting at the table, she doubted they would understand. "I'm sorry to interrupt the evening, but I really feel as though I need to lie down. If you want to stay, Ralph, I'll call a taxi."

"Would you like to lie down here?" Joyce asked.

"Thanks, but I really need to go. I've got two kids waiting for me at home."

"See what I mean," Ralph said smugly, as he reached into his pocket for his keys.

Before leaving, Lisa dutifully thanked the Trentons for dinner and apologized one last time.

"I'll talk to you later," Joyce said, "and I do hope you'll start taking better care of yourself."

Lisa was unusually quiet on the way home as she reflected on the evening's events. Panic closed in on her as she realized she was not cut out to mingle with the Trentons. It wasn't their fault entirely, but she simply wasn't ready to adopt their way of life. Where they were champagne and caviar, she was beer and pizza. What was even more of a shock was the realization she didn't love Ralph enough to want to change. She liked her life, which was more down to earth, exactly the way it was.

She slid a glance at Ralph. Had things escalated beyond her control? Was it too late to back out? After reviewing the events of the evening, Lisa knew she could use a big dose of courage. Throughout her life, whenever it was possible, she had avoided confrontations, but she knew if she continued to act like an ostrich with its head in the sand, she and Ralph would pay for her cowardliness for the rest of their lives.

"Ralph, we need to talk."

Ralph reached over and patted her arm. "It can wait until tomorrow, when your headache is gone."

Her bravery wavering, Lisa accepted Ralph's offer of postponement. "Yes, we'll talk tomorrow."

Ralph pulled up in front of her place and turned off the motor. "Perhaps we can have lunch tomorrow," he said reaching for her.

Just as his lips touched hers Lisa noticed a light on in the unit next door. As she jerked her head for a better look, Ralph's kiss slid from her lips to her cheek. "He's back," she practically shouted.

"Who's back?" Ralph snapped.

"My landlord." Unable to hide her concern, Lisa explained about Grant's injury.

Ralph released her from his embrace. "I

take it he's another one of your goodwill projects." His irritation was clearly evident.

"I . . . He has been awfully good to Todd and me," she answered meekly.

Ralph got out and walked around to Lisa's side of the car, opening her door. "Mother's right you know. You can't save the world all by yourself, Lisa."

"Please, Ralph. I really don't want to argue."

He scowled at her. "Neither do I, but you've got to get your priorities straight. When a man is kissing his fiancé he doesn't want her thinking about her landlord."

Lisa winced at Ralph's bluntness as she placed her key in the lock. "Good night, Ralph."

Inside, she was met by an excited Todd. "Guess, what?" He didn't wait for her to answer. "Grant's back."

"I noticed a light on next door," Lisa said trying not to let her enthusiasm show. She had no right to be so pleased about Grant's return, but at the moment her emotions were too confused to discuss Grant with her brother.

"Where's Susan?" she asked, changing the subject.

"She went to bed early," Todd said.

Lisa stepped out of her shoes. "I'm sorry if I seem a little distracted, but I've got a throbbing headache. I really don't feel like talking tonight. Can we talk in the morning?"

"Sure, Sis."

Sleep did not come right away. Lisa's mind continued to replay the evening's events over and over, refusing to give her any peace.

The one bright spot in the whole evening had come when Ralph had brought her home and she noticed the light on in Grant's apartment. In spite of the breach between her and Grant, she had experienced a comforting warmth upon seeing that light. There was no denying she was glad to have him back.

The longer Lisa mulled things over in her mind, the clearer they became. She not only needed to tell Ralph she couldn't marry him, but she also needed to be honest with herself. She loved Grant. But was she capable of loving him and accepting his job at the same time? And more importantly, was Grant willing to take a chance on her again?

## Chapter Eleven

Lisa stepped from her morning shower and toweled off. Her mood was upbeat. Having made up her mind to approach Grant her emotional state was much improved and under control. She was looking forward to being on speaking terms with him again, and to be held in his arms. Surely, if he loved her, he'd be willing to compromise about his job...just a little. She wouldn't ask him to give up law enforcement altogether, just change departments. There must be some kind of desk work he could do where he wouldn't be out on the streets ducking bullets.

She dressed in a pair of navy slacks and a raspberry pink summer sweater. The deep

167

pink of the sweater heightened the happy glow of her cheeks. Glancing at her watch, she decided she had about thirty minutes before she needed to wake Susan. Lisa grabbed her lipstick. If she hurried she'd have enough time to see Grant before she had to leave for work.

She quickly dabbed on some lipstick then brushed her hair back, tying it with a raspberry ribbon. She was taking a final look in the mirror when she heard the va-room of Grant's sports car coming to life.

Lisa hurried into the living room, hoping to catch Grant before he left, but by the time she got the door unlocked he already had the sports car backed out of the driveway. There wasn't even time to call out before his car was moving down the street.

Disappointed, she stood there as if expecting him to return. When he didn't she reached out, her hand trembling and closed the door. Their talk would have to wait.

Her plans thwarted, Lisa decided she might as well wake Susan. The little girl was using a roll-away bed wedged into a corner of Lisa's bedroom.

When Lisa looked down at the sleeping child her pulse quickened. Susan's face was flushed. Lisa gently placed her hand on the child's forehead. Her fears were confirmed; Susan had a fever.

Susan stirred, opening her eyes as Lisa withdrew her hand. "I don't feel so good."

Trying not to overreact, Lisa patted Susan's hand. "I think I'd better take your temperature."

Lisa heaved a sigh of relief when she removed the thermometer from Susan's mouth. The child's temperature was only slightly above normal. *Probably a summer cold.* "I don't think it's serious, but I think you should stay home from story time today."

"Do I have to?"

Lisa pushed the wisps of hair back from the child's face. "We want you to get over this 'bug' as soon as possible so you'll be able to visit your mother. As long as you're sick I'm afraid you'll have to stay home from the hospital too."

Disappointment flashed across the child's face, but she said nothing.

Lisa squeezed the little girl's hand. Story time and visiting her mother were the highlights of Susan's week. "Don't worry, you'll probably be feeling better in a day or two, and when I come home this afternoon I'll read to you." Susan's face brightened with a tiny smile.

"But you've got to promise me you'll stay in bed today. Or if you want you can move out to the sofa and watch TV. Todd will be here if you need anything, and I'll call later to see how you're doing." Lisa knelt down and straightened out the bedding. "Will you do that for me?"

"Yes."

"Good. I knew I could count on you," Lisa said, turning to go. At the doorway she paused. "I'll make some juice and be back with a glass in a few minutes."

There was no help for it, but it looked like it was going to be one of *those* days, Lisa decided, shaking her head, as she made her way down the hall.

Susan was asleep by the time Lisa returned with the juice, so she quietly placed the glass on the nightstand. As she closed the door to the bedroom a noise sounded from the kitchen.

Hurrying into the kitchen Lisa found Todd, still half asleep, sweeping up some spilled dry cereal. His groggy condition made his efforts almost useless as he tried corralling the yellow, red, and green balls of corn.

"Good morning sleepy head," Lisa greeted him. "Why don't you let me finish cleaning this mess up?"

Todd needed no coaxing and handed over the broom and watched.

In seconds Lisa had the spilled cereal cleaned up and discarded. After directing Todd to a chair she set a glass of juice in front of him then made herself a cup of coffee. Todd downed the juice in one big swallow and held out his glass for more.

Lisa poured him a refill. "Looks like your day is starting like mine."

Todd gave her a puzzled look. "How's that?"

She shrugged her shoulders. "Things just aren't going the way I planned. Susan's coming down with a cold and can't go with me today for one thing."

Todd emptied his second glass of juice. "No problem. I haven't got any plans. I'll hang around and keep an eye on her."

"You won't go next door to visit Grant and forget about her will you?" Lisa asked.

"Don't worry. I can't."

"You can't what?"

"Visit Grant. He won't be here."

"How do you know that?" She didn't think Todd was up when Grant left this morning.

Todd yawned. "Because Grant said so last night. He's got some business to take care of today, and then he's returning to the beach."

Her heart sank. *Leaving again.* He couldn't leave. She needed to talk to him. She glared at her brother. "Why didn't you tell me this last night?"

"Geez, you don't have to be so huffy. You said you didn't feel like talking last night, because of your headache. Remember?"

"You're right, Todd. I'm sorry," Lisa apologized. "It's just been such an annoying morning. I didn't mean to snap at you, but I was hoping to see Grant."

Todd scowled at his sister and reached for the box of cereal. "He left a note for you."

"He did?" Lisa's hopes rose.

Todd finished pouring the colored balls of cereal into his bowl. "I'll go get it."

Lisa accepted the sealed envelope Todd handed her. Excusing herself to the living room she made herself comfortable on the sofa. Her fingers shook with anticipation as she tore open the envelope and removed Grant's letter.

It only took a moment to go over the contents. It was short and to the point. She read it again.

*Lisa,*

*I've been thinking about selling the duplex. If you want to stay, I'll insist the new owner(s) allow you to continue renting your unit.*

*I'll be heading back to the beach sometime today. I just wanted you to know so you wouldn't be surprised when you see a for sale sign go up in the yard.*

*Best of luck,*

*Grant*

The paper slipped from Lisa's hand. *He wasn't coming back.* She was stunned. All her worry about what to say to him had been for nothing. She wasn't going to get a chance. The pain in her heart was mirrored by the sting in her eyes as she fought back tears.

Evidently Grant had accepted their falling out as final and was having no second thoughts. For him it was over.

Folding the note, Lisa returned it to its envelope and tucked it into her handbag.

Her first emotion was anger. How could he be so insensitive to just walk away like this? Didn't he love her?

Lisa sighed heavily. Deep down she knew Grant wasn't to blame for their situation.

She was the one who had insisted they weren't right for each other. Grant had only taken her at her word. Still, she was glad she hadn't embarrassed herself by asking him to give her a second chance. His rejection would have made her misery twice as painful. But painful or not, life went on. If Grant had no regrets, then she could be just as strong. It might take some time, but she would get over him.

Across the room the telephone rang, jogging Lisa from her glum state.

When she heard Ralph's voice on the other end of the line she couldn't believe her misfortune. Hadn't she had enough problems to deal with in one morning? Quickly she chastised herself. Poor Ralph had been a victim too. She had unintentionally used him. She had almost been willing to forego love for security. She felt ashamed.

"How about lunch today?" Ralph asked. "Then we can check out that ring set in Mother and Father's safety deposit box."

How to tell him? Lisa cleared her throat. She didn't want to hurt Ralph, but she didn't want to give him any false hopes. Perhaps the candid truth was best. "I'm sorry, Ralph, but I can't marry you. I—I don't think we're suited for one another, and I don't love you."

Ralph took her news admirably. "As a matter of fact, I thought there might be more to this good neighbor stuff than you were willing to admit last night."

"It isn't my neighbor," Lisa added hastily. "I just don't feel we're right for each other." Ralph's lack of emotion at her announcement eased her guilt considerably.

There was a long pause at the other end of the line. Then Ralph spoke. "Perhaps you're right, Lisa. Maybe we don't have enough in common to make a marriage work. You certainly didn't appear to be enjoying yourself last night."

Lisa grimaced. Had she been that obvious?

"Do you want some time to think this over?" Ralph asked.

"No. I'm not going to change my mind."

"I guess I should admire your honesty, Lisa."

"Thanks for understanding, Ralph. And would it help if I returned your engagement present?"

"That's not necessary."

"I insist."

In spite of all the interruptions, Lisa arrived at the church on time, but when she saw Mattie, her head in her lap, sitting on the front steps Lisa checked her watch. When she realized she was on time she panicked.

Something was wrong. Setting the brake on her car, she rushed over to her friend. Mattie's face was streaked with tears. "Mattie-Mattie, what is it?"

It took a second for Mattie to gain control of her emotions so she could speak. "Look ...look what someone did," she managed between sobs.

Lisa looked at the entrance of the church. The door was hanging haphazardly by one hinge. "Oh," she gasped and moved in the direction of the gapping hole.

Mattie grabbed her arm, stopping her. "It's awful," she warned.

Lisa glanced towards the entryway then back at Mattie. "Are they still here?"

Mattie shook her head.

"Are you all right?" Lisa inquired. "They didn't hurt you, did they?"

Again Mattie shook her head. "I think it happened sometime during the night."

"Have you notified the police?"

Big tears threatened to spill from Mattie's eyes. "No, I've been too stunned to move."

Lisa gently restrained Mattie as her friend attempted to stand. "I'll do it."

On shaky legs, Lisa began her ascent up the stairs. With each step her heartbeat rang louder in her ears.

When she reached the doorway she had to will herself to go on. Pushing past the leaning wood she stepped inside. "Omigosh!" She knew it was going to be bad, but this...this was more than she expected. The tables in the foyer had been broken, but the worst damage had been done in the sanctuary.

The wooden pews had been turned over, and torn hymnals and defaced artwork lay scattered about. Then, as a final insult, paint had been sprayed throughout the room.

A wave of nausea rose in Lisa's throat. Turning, she made her way back outside to civilization and fresh air. It took several deep breaths for her to calm down. When she had regained her composure she realized she hadn't called the police, but her legs refused to budge. She would not—could not—go back inside.

Instead, she returned to where Mattie was seated. "I'll find a phone booth and call the police. Will you be all right while I'm gone?"

"Yes," came Mattie's muffled answer.

Lisa gave Mattie an encouraging smile before leaving. Two blocks from the church Lisa found a phone booth and made her call. She was back at Mattie's side within minutes. "The police should be here soon."

"I can't understand how anyone could do this," Mattie said, her voice cracking. "We'll have to cancel story time today. We haven't time to clean things up before the children start arriving."

Lisa could think of nothing to say. Instead, she placed her arm around Mattie's shoulders and hugged her. She knew how difficult it would be for Mattie to cancel the new project. Convincing the community there was a need for the free program for the underprivileged had been an uphill battle.

Then, before Lisa had time to really think about what she was saying, the words, "We won't cancel," came tumbling from her mouth.

Mattie's deep mahogany gaze met Lisa's blue eyes. "We won't?"

As Lisa recalled, there were three wooden picnic tables in the fenced back yard. If they weren't damaged everything should work out fine. "No, we'll hold it outside."

Mattie looked skeptical. "Maybe . . . it might work."

"Sure it will," Lisa asserted. "Let me go check out the back yard." When she returned she wore a big smile. "We'll call today our picnic day."

Before Mattie could answer a patrol car pulled up to the curb. Two officers got out and walked over to where Lisa and Mattie were standing.

"Are you the one who called in the report?" The officer directed her question at Lisa.

"Yes I am, but Mattie here is the one who was first on the scene."

As the two officers began questioning Mattie, Lisa excused herself. "I'll be in the back yard if you need me for anything."

After retrieving her book bag from her car she hurried around the side of the building. The children would be arriving in about fifteen minutes.

Although she tried concentrating on the job at hand, Lisa's mind kept wandering to the destruction done to the church. Life was so unpredictable and unfair at times. Still, a person couldn't let fears and doubts ruin their life. Like she did with Grant, she added as an afterthought.

Ignoring the ache in her heart that Grant's name caused, Lisa forced her attention back to the book of fairy tales in her hand. She was soon so engrossed in the book that she paid little notice to the approaching footsteps, but the familiar 'hello' caused her to start.

Turning, she was astonished to find Grant standing just a few feet from her. She was unable to keep the surprise out of her voice. "What...what are you doing here?" She couldn't help noticing how good he looked. The days at the beach had given him a golden tan. He looked completely recovered from his injuries.

"I was in the downtown precinct saying goodbye to some buddies when your call came in. I just wanted to make sure you were all right."

Lisa looked up into Grant's warm hazel eyes. *How should she answer his question? Yes, she was all right except for her broken heart, but maybe he didn't want to hear this.*

She changed the subject. "I thought you were leaving town?"

"I am—I was." He paused, letting out a quiet sigh. "Lisa we need to talk."

"I know," she whispered, as he held out his arms.

She flew willingly into his embrace. "Are you okay?" he asked.

She smiled up at him. "Yes, I'm okay if you don't count my broken heart."

"That's good," Grant murmured against her hair. His next words healed all of her pain. "I love you and I've been miserable without you." His mouth sought hers. "Tell me you love me, too," he pleaded.

"Oh, Grant, I love you, and I've been miserable too. I was so afraid I wouldn't see you again." Tears of happiness flowed from her eyes.

Grant gently brushed them away. "I'll see if I can transfer to an office job," he said before kissing her again. "Then we'll be married."

As his words gradually penetrated her brain Lisa pulled back. "No."

Grant's forehead drew together in a frown. "What do you mean, no? Aren't you going to marry me?"

"Yes, of course, I'm going to marry you, but I don't want you to change jobs. It wouldn't be right."

Pleasure erased the frown upon Grant's face. "Are you sure?"

Lisa's smile matched Grant's. "Yes, I'm sure. I'll always worry about you, but I've suddenly realized there are no promises or guarantees in this life for any of us."

Two months later the Inner-City Community Church, refurbished, and decorated with ribbons and flowers, looked better than new as Lisa walked down the aisle in her long white wedding gown to become Grant Harper's bride. Beth, dressed in a stylish lavender dress, made a beautiful maid of honor, and Todd, as best man, looked handsome and older than his years. Susan, in a pink and lavender dress, made a lovely flower girl as her mother and Mattie watched from their seats, smiles on their faces.